I0638185

A Moonlit Serenade

The Seattle Sound Series
Book 8

by Alexa Padgett

A Moonlit Serenade © 2017 Alexa Padgett

Edited by Deborah Nemeth and Nicole Pomeroy
Cover Art by Sarah Hansen of Okay Creations

ISBN: 978-1-945090-21-9

Also by Alexa Padgett

The Seattle Sound Series

Sweet Solace

Between Breaths

Hold You Close

Many Sounds of Silence

From the First

Striker's Waltz

When We Fell Down

A Moonlit Serenade

Moonshine Eyes

The Echo Series

The Spirit Seducer

The Magician's Ruins

The Curse of Kuskurza

Demons & Ultimatums

For Nicole, my editor extraordinaire.
I adore working with you.

CHAPTER ONE
Ryn

"I'm supposed to meet with Ryn Hudson. You know, the songwriter."

"That's me," I said, looking up. Sweet jelly jiggles. I tried to pry my eyes away from those striking hazel eyes, the crooked brown brows, but I couldn't. His was the face of an angel—until panic flamed in his eyes and he lost all the color behind his sexy tan.

"No way. No." He even stumbled back. Like my studio was some type of horror show.

"Excuse me?" I said, hands dropping to my hips. Good thing my guitar was hooked around my neck by its strap. Otherwise, four thousand dollars' worth of handmade Taylor would be on the ground, dented, possibly broken.

"Ryn's a songwriter. A *musician*," he stressed the last word, his accent was strong. Not British, I didn't think. Unless it was Cockney. But he didn't sound like Adele, the only person whose voice I'd ever heard with that accent.

"I'm aware of what I am. Thank you very much."

"But you…you're playing chords for babies."

I glanced around my class, shocked to see all ten moms and their kids staring, just as awestruck by the man as I'd been moments before. Before he ticked me off.

"That's what we do. Play songs for the kids so they learn about pitch and rhythm. Well, in this case, we played 'Jingle Bells' because the song rocks, and it's close to Christmas."

"Oh," Helena moaned. "I think I'm going to die. I knew I should've combed my hair."

I glanced over at her, nonplussed by her drama. Her daughter Ilona sucked on her pacifier in slow, deep pulls, eyes lowered to dangerous, prenap-time levels.

"You're Jake Etsam," Stephani yelped. I didn't appreciate the predatory look in her eyes when she glanced at the angel-man. He'd asked for *me*. Ergo, he was mine.

Whoa. Hold the shaky eggs. Where had that thought come from?

"Oops, Kendall had a little problem there, Steph," I said, not trying to hide the laughter from my voice.

Stephani half moaned, half shrieked as Kendall upchucked more of her milk straight down Steph's low-cut, clingy top, her face as red as the poinsettias I'd placed on the top shelves of the bookcases in my room. A few of the other moms choked back giggles as Stephani hopped up. Clutching the baby, she raced out the door, past the angel-man named Jake—as in Jake Etsam, bassist of Jackaroo, the world's most famous band—toward the bathrooms at the end of the long hall.

"Guess that's a wrap for the day," Helena said, gathering up Ilona in her arms. The fifteen-month-old grunted, her eyes slamming shut. "You wore this one out, Ryn. Thanks for a great class of singing and songwriting," she said. The frown she threw over her shoulder at Jake did not register in the man's demeanor.

"Bye-bye!" Lionel shrieked. His mother, Kim, winced and smiled, her expression somewhere between apologetic and kill-me-now. "Transitions," she said.

"You're right, Lion-man. We didn't sing our goodbye song. You want a shaky egg to jam with?"

Lionel barreled through two other kids, sending them flying

as he dug into the egg basket, his mother chastising him and apologizing to the other moms at the same time.

Yeah, Jake Etsam, angel-man and rock god. This is *my* music scene. Deal with it.

I strummed out the chord and Lionel bounced, his diaper-clad tush mere inches from the carpet as he got busy to his favorite song. Ilona popped her head up and threw herself from her mother's arms to get in on the shaky-egg action. Samuel and Petey stopped crying as I started singing, each clapping and matching my pitch as we worked through each of their names to say goodbye.

"And hug your mommy tight. Bye-bye till next week," I said. I set my guitar in the middle of the floor, wincing a little as the remaining toddlers swarmed toward the polished wood, attacking the strings with their tiny fingers. This was their favorite part of the class and an easy way for the moms to pry the other chunky, plastic musical instruments from the kids' small hands.

"That's a custom-made Taylor," Jake choked. He'd moved behind me as we sang the final song. Well, the kids and I sang. The rest of the women eyed Jake's progress as he tiptoed around the edge of the classroom.

"I'd heard your brother was spending time in Seattle while his girlfriend recovered," Joan said. She was the oldest of our group—little Carina had been a surprise for Joan, her husband, and her high-school-aged daughter. She tucked her thick salt-and-pepper hair behind her ears as she set Carina down next to my guitar. The toddler cooed and slammed her palm against the strings.

"Fiancée," Jake replied, eyes still on the four toddlers climbing onto my guitar. "You're not worried about them breaking it?"

"Not really, no. They just want to look inside to see where the sound comes from."

"My daughter's a big fan of yours," Joan continued.

Jake raised startled eyes. Joan shook her head on a laugh. "Not this little cutie. My older daughter. She's a junior in high school."

"Oh, right-o. Want me to sign something for her?"

"Would you?" Joan asked, her smile blooming larger than I'd ever seen it. "That would just make Nicole's year."

"Course." Jake snagged a pen from the shelf behind me before grabbing an early-childhood music pamphlet and scrawling his name across the front. "Cheers." He handed the brochure to Joan, who clutched it to her chest. No way she was giving that to her daughter.

The other moms asked for his autograph, too. After another fifteen minutes, the toddlers had all lost interest in my guitar and two of them were bawling in earnest while Ilona and Petey rubbed their eyes and yawned.

"Nap time," Helena said. "Nice to meet you, Jake. Maybe if you stop by again, you can sing with Ryn. She has an amazing voice." Even I heard the reprimand in her words.

Jake dipped his head. "I know. Pulled me in with the first note."

My gaze darted back to his, and when our eyes locked, sincerity burned from the depths of his hazel eyes.

Lionel hugged my leg, breaking my intense contact with Jake. I ruffled Lionel's hair, then I waved a last goodbye to the ladies and kids. As they gathered their diaper bags and coats, I busied myself with wiping the toddler spittle from my guitar and setting it into its case.

"Er, I need to apologize."

My gaze darted back to Jake's. His cheeks and even his neck burned bright red but he kept his eyes firmly on mine. The intensity of his look slid over my body, making my skin warm and soften.

"I'm sorry if I offended you. I didn't mean…I just wasn't expecting…you know."

He stuttered through the apology. I shoved my hands into the back pockets of my jeans. *Of course* I knew who Jake Etsam was. *Of course* I was thrilled he'd sought me out. But that didn't mean I was going to let him trample over my work.

"No, I really don't," I said, shrugging. I snapped the last clasp of my guitar case closed and stood.

Jake ran his hand through his long brown waves. "I'm a wanker," he said, his voice a little lost. "I'm so sorry. Really. I should have thought before I…"

Stephani barreled back into the room, eyes wide. "I'm so glad you're still here!" Her eyes never left Jake's face even as she lowered Kendall to her feet. The nine-month-old's lip quivered but Stephani ignored her, racing to Jake's side and grabbing his arm. "I'm your biggest fan. Omigod! I can't believe I'm, like, touching you."

Jake inclined his head toward the now-sobbing Kendall. "What about your little girl?"

"She's not mine," Stephani said, frowning. "I just watch her. I'm totally single. Will you sign something for me? Want to grab some lunch? A drink? Go to the skating rink over at Westlake Center?"

I leaned my guitar against the wall and bent to pick up Kendall, whose whimpers ratcheted up to full-on wails. I cradled her in my arms and pressed my lips to her ear, singing a lullaby I'd written last year as part of my healing process.

Kendall quieted enough for me to hear Stephani proposition Jake again. Yeah, Steph wasn't ever going to be on my faves list.

I patted Kendall's back and continued to croon, warmth building in my chest as the baby's pretty pink lips parted into a yawn. She looked up at me with her huge brown eyes. She reminded me of an owlet. She blinked, pressing her cheek into my chest.

"Oh, I'm sure Ryn won't mind keeping an eye on Kendall for a while. She loves kids." Stephani dismissed me without a second thought.

I did like Kendall quite a bit. But I wasn't going to change my afternoon plans so that Stephani could bag the sexy Aussie rocker.

Before I could tell her so, Jake smiled—well, it was more of a pained grimace—and sent me a pleading look.

"I'm on Ryn's calendar this arvo. And then I'm off to a meeting. Another time, perhaps."

"Oh. Well. Sure." Stephani's disappointment was palpable. Her eyes lit up. "Want me to show you all the cool places to party tonight? I'm dropping Kendall off at her mom's office around four."

I rolled my eyes but didn't stop singing. Kendall heaved a sigh and closed her eyes.

"Can't. I'm off to dinner at my brother's place. Private. Just family. Mila's still healing."

I chuckled into Kendall's hair. *Way to lay it on thick, angel-man.*

"Here you go, Steph. She's down for the count. Have a fun afternoon." I couldn't resist pressing a kiss to Kendall's soft, pink cheek. If it was anyone else, I would have gladly snuggled the baby for as long as I could. A pang bit through my chest as I swiped my thumb across Kendall's forehead, struggling with the longing I'd felt every time I looked at someone else's child.

This is what I lost when Desden didn't come home from his last tour in Iraq. We'd planned to start a family after I finished my master's degree. Instead, one night two years ago, three Army officers, in full dress attire, knocked on my apartment door to hand me Dez's medal of valor. He died in that war and I've been alone since.

I huffed out a breath and stepped back.

"You 'right?" Jake's voice softened as he stepped closer. Since his initial outburst, Jake had been considerate—not just of my feelings but of those of the ladies in my class.

"Yeah." I hoped. I'd learned grief hit like this—a sudden sucker punch to the chest. But I'd also learned to breathe through the intensity because I'd already come out the other side. Maybe scarred, but living my life nonetheless.

Such as it was. *So* different from what I'd hoped.

"Mila looks like that when she sees a baby. My brother's fiancée."

I met Jake's concerned, intense hazel eyes. His hair tumbled into messy waves. Like he'd let it air dry after a morning surf. Or rolled out of a lover's bed.

Whoa. Where had that thought come from?

"I never lost a child, like Mila, if that's what you're getting at."

"Figured you knew who I am, read all the news about my family like the rest of the world," he said, his dimples flashing. They were deep wells bracketing his mouth like extra commas. Dez's dimples were smaller, just hints at humor. But, Jake, I'd bet, lived larger than my deceased war-hero husband ever had.

The pain settled low in my stomach, same as it did every time I heard of another's pregnancy. I'd begged Dez to try for our own child in the short months between his deployments. Often. He'd said he'd talk about baby matters when he returned from his next tour.

"Congratulations to your brother and his fiancée," I muttered.

He eyed me, aware of my less-than-enthusiastic response. "So that's why I'm here. Partly anyway. I heard your lullaby. It's gorgeous."

I'd had a fantasy of Dez's dark head singing to my growing bump. Well, except for the fact Dez barely held a tune, and he'd never been interested in music, preferring to kayak or rock climb—some physical outdoorsy activity that ate up his energy.

"Thanks."

Jake fidgeted, flustered by my lack of enthusiasm. "So, I thought, well, maybe you and I could sing it. I wanted to give it to Mila and Murphy as a wedding gift. They're getting married in February, weekend after Valentine's Day. Probably so Murphy doesn't fuck up and forget both."

I smiled, surprised by how touched I was by the thoughtfulness of the gesture. Jake Etsam might be a rock star, but he loved his family. I bet he'd make a great dad.

Flipping hyenas. I forced my eyes away from the all the gorgeous hotness standing in front of me. And that accent—swoon worthy—no wonder my ovaries had replaced my brain.

"That's sweet. So, you want to record the lullaby."

He fidgeted again. "I'd really like to sing with you. As a duet." His eyes darted around the room, his cheeks turning a ruddier hue. "But I don't sing, normally."

"You did back up on 'She's So Bad.'"

He smiled, probably thrilled I knew that. I almost rolled my eyes. Everyone knew Jackaroo. They were *the* band of the year—maybe the decade.

"Right-o. Also for 'Between Breaths.' But that's because both of those were on-the-fly, last-minute additions to the set list."

"You're kidding?" I gaped. I couldn't help it. "Those—both of those—are multiplatinum recordings!"

Jake shrugged, shoving his hands in his pockets. "Only bigger hit was 'Hold You Close,' which Murph insisted on singing solo. Those tunes are full of real emotion. That's what the fans respond to."

"On the fly?" I gasped, unable to comprehend his words afterward. But if Jake connected with my lullaby, then he'd felt the pent-up yearning in my song for the child I'd yet to meet.

"That may be overstating it. But point is, I'm not a singer, though I can carry a tune well enough. *You* are a singer. And I'd like to do an entire album for Mila. I think she'll like this as a gift, especially after everything she's been through in the past couple of years."

A sensitive, caring man. They weren't as rare as unicorns, but as much as I'd loved Dez, I had to admit he hadn't been the sensitive type. Unless… "Are you in love with her?" The question was sharp and inappropriate. Still, I wasn't helping a man steal his brother's pregnant lover.

"With Mila?" His eyes widened, turning greener than gold. I braced myself for him to say something scathing then turn and walk out. I rocked back on my heels, surprised when he shook

ALEXA PADGETT

his head, chuckling. "No. She's always been like my big sister. It's just...Valentine's Day is her favorite holiday, and I want her to be, you know, happy. Because Murph is, and believe me, Murphy happy is a big deal. Fair dinkum."

Not quite sure about all that, but he seemed genuine. "Oh. Okay."

Those dimples popped back out. "Odd way to ask if I'm single."

"I wasn't." My cheeks flamed. "I just didn't want to help you romance away your brother's fiancée."

"With lullabies for my brother's bub?" He eyed me, a small smirk lingering at the corner of his mouth. "That'd be a new one."

"You're laughing at me," I huffed. His eyes crinkled at the corners. My chest burned, and I exhaled before I became too lightheaded. Dez was a handsome man, but Jake had looks and... presence. That's what made him so good of a performer. That I-don't-care-what-you-think vibe and sexy-as-sin smile.

"Because you're funny."

I picked up my guitar case and started toward the door, face flaming with embarrassment and inexplicable tears welling in my eyes.

"Wait." His voice filled with panic. "D-don't go," he stuttered.

I blinked back the tears—good at it after so much practice. "I'm not sure we have anything further to discuss."

"The song...maybe an album."

"I don't do vanity projects. I'm happy working with the early-childhood music program."

"This wouldn't be for vanity," he said with a gentle touch to my arm to turn me back toward him. "And I'm sure you're quite successful with your program. I've heard you sing." He smiled, those dimples flashing again, but his eyes remained uncertain.

I must stop melting each time he smiled. Who knew I had such a soft spot for *cheeks*?

"Thanks for popping in, Jake. Good luck with the project. I'll sign for the use of 'A Moonlit Serenade.'"

He grabbed the guitar case's handle, his warm hand sliding over mine. I jolted, letting go. My hand still tingled, the warmth drifting up my arm, into my chest, pooling low in my groin.

Fantastic. The first man I'd been attracted to in *years*, and he had to be a celebrity. One who managed to make me feel small and insignificant.

There was no way meeting Jake Etsam could end in anything other than embarrassment or heartache.

CHAPTER TWO
Jake

Never had I wanted to be as smooth with the ladies than I did right now, with Ryn—a long-standing problem for me, the shy, stuttering art nerd. I might've gotten over the stutter, mostly, but I'd never learned how to talk to a woman I was interested in. In fact, my typical way of dealing with such as situation was to run away or, rarer still, kiss the woman so she wouldn't realize I was more frightened to talk to her.

I couldn't do that with Ryn Hudson—didn't know how to seduce her to my whims like Murphy could. Then again, I had a lot more on the line than a simple song—no one expected me to manage a project of this size and do it well. Just like no one understood why I'd be willing to use the funds from this album to subsidize the gallery I wanted to open. Not that I planned to tell this woman about my plans and goals. I mean, I wanted to, but she was already angry with me.

I'd mucked this whole thing up.

I tipped up her chin and stared her beautiful eyes—a light brown offset by all that long, thick, blond hair. She overwhelmed me.

What were we talking about? Right. Her song.

"I don't want you to sign over rights. I'd never ask you to do something like that. I'm working with Asher Smith to build something beautiful. He's going to produce the album."

"You know Asher Smith, too?" she asked, a little quiver—of longing?—sliding into her voice.

"Yeah. Hayden Crewe, our lead singer? He's married to Asher's sister-in-law."

Her soft lips—petal pink and glossy—pulled together. Blimey, her lips were pretty. I wanted to run my thumb over them. Then my tongue. Nibble at the corners before swooping in for a long, thorough taste.

"Do you people ever date, let alone marry, normal people?"

"What do you mean by 'you people'?" I hedged. Up until two years ago, I sat in the normal group. Growing up with an absentee dad and a single mum didn't make for lots of extras in anything.

"Famous. Rich. Is there some code that you have to keep the world's wealth up there, in that top tier?"

I blinked at her, surprised by the strength of her disgust. Most people—scratch that, nearly everyone I met—turned awestruck. So Ryn's irritation surprised me. "Er, that's a no."

I'd spent the last few minutes of her class sizing her up—athletic build, taller than average. Probably five-seven. With that bloody mane of sexy blond waves. Light brown brows that arched with salon perfection over those bright eyes that looked at the children in her class with love and patience. Pert nose, sweet pink lips made for kissing. A small, rounded chin. Slightly pointed ears.

She looked like a Northwestern version of Boticelli's Venus. Maybe a da Vinci sketch of *La Scapigliata*, one of my favorites. Ryn was feisty as, but with that sexy girl-next-door vibe I adored. Approachable—except not now. Her expression turned mulish.

Ah, a stubborn streak. Little did she know I did well working 'round stubborn. Grew up with Murphy, didn't I?

"So, you people seek out the poor minions and marry up sweet, middle class girls in a fairytale?"

"There's no way for me to answer that question and look like a reasonable human being, let alone a decent bloke."

She blew out a breath hard enough to shift the blond bangs from her forehead. "You're right. I'm sorry. It's just…you weren't very nice when you walked into my room earlier, and I'm defensive."

Even though I wanted to look aside, I forced my eyes to stay locked on hers. "Point. I apologize again. I didn't know, er…"

"Early-childhood music," she supplied.

"Yes. Right-o. That existed. When I called the office to get your details, I assumed you taught college students." I raised my hands. "Since you work at a college."

She dipped her head in a little nod, but crossed her arms over her chest, hugging her waist. Her narrow waist that sat just above that delectable, round bum.

"I'm doing honest work. *Good* work with these kids."

"You are." I'd seen how much the bubs loved it. She'd transformed me into a believer. Could be that her voice seduced me, though. Because, fair dinkum, Ryn Hudson's voice wove a spell. After hearing her today, I *had* to have her on my album.

"They're learning to love music before they can walk. Well, some of them, anyway."

I must have hit a nerve—not the first time she'd defended her work. "You have a gorgeous voice. One of the best I've ever heard. Melodic, clear. That's why I sought you out. I'm sorry if I made you feel like less."

She blinked, her mouth parting just enough for me to see the straight white teeth and her little pink tongue. I shouldn't have the fantasies about that tongue licking all over my chest, down

14

my abdomen…Yeah, now wasn't the time for that. And where the bloody hell had those fantasies come from?

I planned to work with this woman. Ryn was beautiful, but she was prickly as. I didn't handle angry women well. Tended to make me stutter more often, feel stupid and clumsy. So, it was good I just wanted her to sign on to my project, not date her.

Blimey. *Date her?* I hadn't dated a woman…in far too long.

"Wow," she said, her voice small. Her lips tilted up, and I held my breath, desperate to see her face alight with joy. I bet those features would be breathtaking. At least as much as the look of longing when she'd held the baby moments ago.

I'd never seen such loss, such need on someone's face. When this woman felt, it was soul-deep. Life changing.

I wanted her to look at me like that. More, I wanted to deserve that look.

And I had no idea what to do with this meeting, with Ryn. Just that I wasn't ready to leave her company. Not yet. Not till I got what I needed.

Her.

No. That was wrong. Ryn's voice on my album.

And…fine! Bloody hell, I wanted Ryn.

"You do know how to argue your point," she said, her voice quiet as she dropped her gaze.

"Years of art history papers," I blurted.

"Papers?"

I winced. Why the hell would I bring that up? Women expected me to be larger than life, not some art-loving arse. Blimey. My brain slipped behind my bloody mouth when I admitted to wanting her.

"Persuasive research."

She pulled her bottom lip with her thumb and forefinger. "You studied art history?"

In for a penny. Talking to her seemed to be reducing her dislike of me. "I wanted to be a museum curator." I shrugged. "Then the band took off."

"That's fascinating."

She didn't sound fascinated. She glanced at the clock behind her.

"Sorry, but I need to run. I have to eat before my next class at three."

Knowing better than to push my luck, I nodded, unable to trust myself not to stutter. Best to regroup and try again.

"Bye, Jake. Thanks for stopping by."

Her tone offered complete dismissal—not even a chance at redemption. I shoved my hands into my pockets and trudged out the door, head down so as not to draw attention to my red cheeks.

———◆———

"So, you stuffed it yesterday," I muttered to myself.

"You say something, Jake?" Alan, my bodyguard, asked. He and Isaac, my other guard, turned back to look at me. Both were large men who rarely smiled.

"Nothing to worry about," I said. I ran my hand down the back of my neck as I stared out the car window, seeing my reflection and, beyond that, the twenty-four-meter-tall Christmas tree near the Space Needle. Though it was still daylight, the white lights sparkled in the soft winter sunlight. I sighed, loving the hopefulness of the multicolored lights strewn around the edges of

16

all the buildings we passed. Yanks did this holiday up right.

I took a deep breath, happily inhaling the faint scent of cinnamon and cool air that drifted from one of the street vendors selling hot chocolate and winter treats. "Today's a new day. A better one."

Blimey. I hoped so.

"Will you guys wait for me out here?" I asked.

Isaac nodded but Alan frowned, clearly unhappy with my request.

"You know the drill," I said. "You guys make normal people uncomfortable."

"We also keep you safe. What you pay us for," Alan responded, a scowl spreading over his rigid features.

I'd pulled up a copy of Ryn's class schedule from her web page last night and made it to her classroom just as her eleven o'clock let out. I kept my back to the mums, having learned my lesson yesterday.

After peeking into her classroom to ascertain she was alone, I walked through the door. The colorful foam pads cushioned my footfalls.

"Be ready in a minute, Linda," Ryn said from the closet, her back turned toward me. "I'm starving."

Right-o. My in. "Why don't I buy you lunch and tell you about the album?"

Ryn edged back from the closet and looked at me over her shoulder, eyes wide.

"What are you doing here?"

"I came to apologize for my comments yesterday." I gestured toward her. "And buy you a meal."

"Totally unnecessary."

Her stomach answered, grumbling louder before she could tell me she wasn't hungry. She'd planned to do so, I was sure of it.

Smooth was not the word people would ever use with me and the ladies. *Determined* and *unwilling to give up* might be. I needed to focus on my goal. Create this album, change the course of my career to one I wanted. Craved.

And get to know this woman who'd managed to tie me into knots. I spent an extra hour working out yesterday to burn off my embarrassment over my actions. Then spent most of the night trying to forget Ryn's thick, long waves and her soft, pink lips.

I sucked in a breath, willing my body not to respond to the growing excitement such thoughts produced.

"There's a café around the corner. I saw it on my way in. I'd really like to discuss this album with you."

She looked uncertain, so I pressed my advantage.

"It's a free meal. If you don't like my spiel, you can tell me to stuff it."

Her lips flipped up in a small smile.

"Please?"

She turned away, but instead of ignoring me, she set her guitar in the corner and gathered up her down-filled coat. Ushering me from the room, she turned and locked the door, jiggling the handle.

"What about your friend? Linda?"

Ryn shook her head. "We didn't have set plans. I just assumed you were her."

"You could've brought it with you if you were worried about it. That's a nice instrument."

"It is. But it'll be safer here than at a café with us."

"Why use such an expensive guitar for the lessons and risk those nippers damaging it?"

Her lips flattened into a thin line. "My husband bought it for me before his last deployment."

My stride hitched and my chest burned. She was married. *Bloody fucking hell.* "Your husband?" The word weighted my tongue.

She watched me from the corner of her eye, a puff of white drifting from her nose as she exhaled, hard. Blimey, the weather took a dip. "He died in a bomb blast. Iraq."

Wasn't I the world's biggest arse for feeling relief? "That's horrible."

She shivered. From the chill or from the memories? "It was."

"Do you mind if I ask when?"

"Dez died a little more than two years ago."

"But you're so young," I sputtered. "To have been married, I mean." *Shut up, Jake!* My foot was so far in my mouth, I'd never be able to remove it.

"He enlisted when we were nineteen. College wasn't working out for him. He did his first tour at twenty. We were married the month before he left for basic training."

I pushed open the door to the café, my hand above her head as I leaned in, returning to her story. "You don't look much older than twenty-two now."

She smiled as she passed under my arm. "That's a good one. Keep it in your repertoire."

I followed her into the place, irritation licking at my heels. "It wasn't a line," I muttered.

But Ryn didn't hear me; she was already chatting with the hostess. "So, I'll see you and little Isabel on Friday?" she said.

"Wouldn't miss it," the hostess smiled. Her mouth transformed into a little "o" when she saw me, her eyes widening. "You-you didn't tell me you were having lunch with a rock star."

"Oh, is that what he is?" Ryn said. "C'mon, Jen. He's just a guy."

"N-no," she whispered. I shifted, uncomfortable with her devouring gaze. "He's gorgeous, talented, *and* rich."

Ryn shrugged. "Last I checked his name was Jake."

Before I knew it, I'd grabbed her hand and squeezed it, just a little. We both inhaled at the intensity of the connection. Ryn's gaze crashed into mine and held it. My blood pulsed through my temples before thickening through my guts. I saw Ryn's chest rise, then fall once, twice, three times as her pulse slammed against her neck. She dropped my fingers and stepped around me, following Jen. I trailed behind her, my grin wider than a well-fed dingo because no matter how much she wanted to deny the chemistry between us, she couldn't.

Jen cast one last look at me after she set out our menus. Ryn plopped into the booth and began to remove her jacket and the fleece vest she'd worn over a soft, green long-sleeve blouse. I slid into the opposite side, enjoying the residual tingles enough I didn't remove my coat for another moment. I sat it next to me, neatly folded, just as Ryn did with hers.

Ryn leaned forward until her chest touched the table. "Jen likes you."

I leaned forward, too. Our noses, better our lips, nearly touched. "I don't really care."

Eyebrows raised, Ryn leaned back. "You don't like your fans?"

Always searching for a reason to dislike me. Couldn't say I blamed her after my complete muck up yesterday. Ryn must assume I was a pompous arse—much like Murphy's portrayal in the press. This was going to be a tough uphill slog, but Ryn was worth the effort. Her voice—her contribution to the album, I meant.

Bloody hell. I ran my fingers through my hair. I still wanted her. Maybe more today than yesterday.

"My fans, sure. The ones who are interested in my music. But as you said, I'm an actual person, and I prefer to be considered so as opposed to a piece of rich meat."

Ryn puckered her lips, picking up her menu. "Guess we'll have to work on the whole I'm-more-than-a-sex-symbol thing for you."

"Fair dinkum." I perused the menu, unsurprised by the number of Asian-inspired options. The Northwest took its fusion cuisine seriously. "What's good?"

"Pretty much anything. I love the ramen."

"Never had it."

"You're from Sydney, right? Isn't there a lot of Asian influence in the food there? I mean, you're close to Japan, Tahiti, Fiji."

Her breath caught, just a little, at the mention of the islands. Interesting. I nodded my thanks for the water that a harried, middle-aged waitress had set at my elbow before looking back at Ryn. "Got a thing for the islands, eh? Don't rightly know. Growing up, my mum worked too many hours simply to keep a roof over our heads. By the time I was old enough to know different, Murphy and I were used to Mum's cooking. It's traditional: bangers and mash, meat pies, fish and chips when we had the extra cash for

21

a treat. Pizza. Standard American fare, I'd guess."

"Except for the meat pies. I've had a chicken-pot pie. Oh, and shepherd's pie."

"Never had either." The waitress was back so I motioned for Ryn to order. Once she had, I said, "The same," and handed our server my menu.

Ryn sipped her water, eyes never leaving my face.

"So, how old are you?" I asked.

"Twenty-six."

"A mere babe yourself."

Her eyes clouded and she sat back. "Not hardly, thanks to life experience. So…tell me about this album."

Much as I wanted to push, to learn more about her, she'd shut me down yesterday and then again today when I held her hand. From her body language, I'd say she'd do it again. For the best, anyway. I was here with her for business, nothing more.

"Asher's started his own record label here in Seattle."

She raised her brows again, but I couldn't tell if that was a go-on gesture or one of surprise.

"He's looking to put out work that the big labels don't want to touch. All the projects he's dreamed of doing but either didn't have the time or the backing of his band to do."

"Sounds ambitious."

I smiled. "Everything the man does is ambitious. Hitting forty never sounded so good."

"*You* have to celebrate thirty first," Ryn said, and I smiled, pleasure looping though my chest. The casual drop of information was proof enough she'd paid attention to me before now.

"When I told Asher about the idea of the lullabies, he asked me to set it up. He also loved the idea of lullabies for Valentine's Day. Something different, classy, sweet. You know, nonstandard love for a holiday full of romance." I stopped talking, wishing I'd kept my mouth shut. She waited, seeming to know I had more to say. "I'd just heard your song from a friend. She has some baby recordings." *Quit running your jaw, Jake.*

"Must be from the local artist compilation Linda asked me to do."

"I looked you up, found out you were local. And here I am."

We both sat back as large white bowls plunked onto the table in front of us. I stared, bemused by the steaming broth in the bowl.

"Add the chicken and whatever else you want."

"Right-o," I muttered. Smaller white bowls of grilled chicken, scallions, shredded carrots, steamed broccoli, snap peas, soy sauce, and peanuts were next to my large ramen-and-broth bowl. "Peanuts? Chop sticks?" Bloody hell. I'd never used them before.

Ryn had already emptied a few of her smaller bowls into the larger one. She pushed away the peanuts, wrinkling her nose, and picked up the chop sticks. "Everything okay?"

"Don't know. This looks hard."

"Not too hard for a world-famous rock star, surely." She looked down to grab a bite of noodles with her chopsticks.

She'd bought the hype, the image the label set. I nearly snorted at the irony of her take of me. As the shy, bookish Etsam brother, I'd learned to play the bass when Murphy needed more help with his guitar and music studies. Once Murphy met Hayden Crewe at uni, making music went from hobby to serious work. Thankfully, our real break didn't come until I'd finished my courses.

In all those years, I'd always been the least interesting member of our four-member band. I was the quiet bloke who'd act as one of his mate's wingman for yet another bar troll. Not that I didn't like women—I did, but casual chat-ups defied my abilities. And being raised by a single woman who was strong enough to make the transition from homemaker to manager showed me the traits I wanted in my future partner.

After another long moment of nervous staring, I picked up the chop sticks. Dipping them into the broth, I fought to gather up a few slippery noodles. At Ryn's giggle, I looked up.

"It's messy, but it's worth it. Promise."

With a shrug, I shoved the chop sticks into my mouth. The tang from the broth mixed with the slight nutty flavor of the pasta. I chewed slowly, nodding. "Nice."

"They use buckwheat flour. For the noodles."

"Is that why it tastes different?"

"Yes."

Ryn scooped up another bite, unconcerned by the slight slurping noise she made to pull the noodles into her mouth. She chewed, still watching me.

"Are you going to eat? We could get you something else if you don't like it."

Warmth filled me. It wasn't often people worried about my needs. Most of the time, especially with the few women I dated, they expected me to take care of them. I didn't mind, really, but it wasn't as though I were a mind-reader. Half the time, the ladies stormed off, their irritation as obvious as their lipstick.

Ryn wore no lippy. She was gorgeous with those laughing sherry eyes and damp pink lips devoid of anything other than broth.

I looked down into my bowl, managed to bring up another bite.

Up to now, I'd muddled along. Not unhappy with my lot but never seeking to move into the limelight. I was young—just twenty-eight myself—and good enough to look at.

But I wasn't the pretty-boy frontman like Hayden Crewe, and Murphy owned the bad-boy vibe.

Even this project was more about my family than finding my own fame. I just didn't crave it. When I took stock of my life, I wanted simple, easy dreams.

But, like everything else, the opportunity for me to work at a gallery and come home to a sweet wife each night blew up when "She's So Bad" went multiplatinum. "Between Breaths" propelled us even higher. Honestly, I'd never have to work again and be fine. But I wasn't the type to settle in because I could.

For the first time in my career, I *wanted* something. I wanted Ryn. Her voice for the songs, but if I was honest with myself, I was attracted to her. Even after my blundered beginning she'd allowed me to stick around.

And I wanted to.

The album was the perfect excuse to keep her close enough until I talked her into a date.

CHAPTER THREE
Ryn

"Did you enjoy your lunch?" I asked, leaning back against the vinyl cushion. Small white Christmas lights were woven between the booths, the main pendants turned down to give the space a cozier feel. The restaurant had cleared out and the noise level dropped.

Jake hesitated. "It was different."

My good mood collapsed. "I shouldn't suppose everyone likes what I do." Dez liked ramen—he'd been the one to turn me on to the dish. He'd made it for me about once a week after our marriage, and we'd laughed as we slurped the noodles.

I rubbed my chest at the memory. Maybe spending time with Jake was a mistake.

Jake responded quickly. I'd noticed that about him. He didn't like me to feel bad. "Not at all. It's just that I'm Aussie. I love Vegemite sandwiches. Traveling took some getting used to."

He'd paid the bill. After wiping his mouth and hands one last time, he set his napkin under the edge of his bowl. "You ready?"

"Sure. But you didn't tell me any more about the album."

"You said you had another class at two. It's just before now."

I jumped up. "Thanks for keeping an eye on the time! I need to get back. This group is older and a couple of the moms show up about fifteen minutes before to chat."

"Let's get you back then."

Much as I liked his gentlemanly door holding, part of me wished he'd try to grab my hand again. Those tingles… yeah, I'd like them again.

In weeks, I would hit the three years since Dez and I caressed one another. So many years too long for intimate contact.

Jake and I walked down the street, not quite touching. Was I wrong? I'd thought he was attracted to me, but maybe I'd misread the signals. I was so out of touch with the whole dating scene. That's what happened when your first boyfriend morphed into your husband.

I waited for a cyclist to pass. With a quick check back to the right, I stepped onto the crosswalk. "Watch it!" Jake grabbed me, yanking me back up the curb. My ankle caught on the concrete, and I fell back against him. We landed in a heap of tangled limbs as a red sedan tore through the red light.

"Bloody stupid bugger," Jake muttered. He winced as he stood. "Are you hurt?"

"I don't think so." I took his hands and let him pull me back to my feet. My ankle was tender with road rash but I could put weight on it.

"Came out of nowhere, he did."

"Thanks for pulling me back in time."

"Glad I was there to do so." Jake's brows were still scrunched as he glared through the light.

This time, he didn't drop my hand as he walked next to me all the way to the door of my building.

"Give me your number, and I'll give you mine. I'd really like to talk more about the project."

I weighed my choices. Spending time with Jake proved nicer than I anticipated. And, though I had pride in my work, turning down a chance to work with some of the biggest names in music stank of stupidity. I met his gaze, taking in those patient hazel eyes.

He handed me his phone, and I typed in my number.

"Um. Where are you staying?"

Jake grimaced. "At a hotel for the moment."

"Not your scene?"

"Nah. I'm a homebody. My mum said if I wasn't in a band, she'd have to pry me out of the house."

I handed him back his phone. It was sleek, the newest version. With more reluctance, I dropped my much older model into his hand.

He opened the contacts and typed away. Handing it back, he met my eyes. "Dinner?"

No. "I'm busy tonight." Thank goodness for that, because my emotions were a tangled mess of desire for him and a desire to remember Dez and our years together.

Disappointment filled his gaze. "Tomorrow then?"

He wasn't going to let this go. I glanced away, unsure how best to handle him.

The rest of the week was a safer subject than my plans for tonight. "I'm helping my colleague with a new composition for her class. I'm going to be here until after six most nights this week."

Hope lit those eyes, causing the green specks to spark brighter. My heart thumped in my chest.

"After then? How about seven thirty?"

I wanted this man. And, in some strange twist of fate, he seemed to want me.

"I can't." *See you again. Take you up on your offer.* My nose stung as I blinked back tears.

"You sure about that?"

"Yes," I said. I dropped my phone back into the large tote I carried. "I need to go." I sighed, hating how torn Jake made me feel.

He hesitated as his eyes met mine. Then, he leaned in, his lips brushing against my cheek. Just a casual exchange many people had throughout their day, but I held my breath, shocked and dizzy from his nearness. His scent slammed into my head, setting off all kinds of responses. My body heated, my belly zinged. Holy cow. I really wanted this man. *Really.*

I pulled back and glanced at his lips. Soft. Perfect. I wanted them on mine. Before I could think, he'd stepped back, hands shoved into his pockets.

"I'll be in touch."

My hand to my cheek, I watched him walk away. I wanted him to. But, more, I wanted him to overcome my misgivings. I wanted him to want me *that* much. I wrapped my arms around my middle as I tried to hold in the building disappointment.

"He's yummy, Ryn."

I turned to smile at Linda—a music theory professor I shared the floor with, and a friend.

"He is."

She tipped her head, ash-blond hair spilling over her shoulder. "So why don't you look happy?"

Good question. Not one with an easy answer. At least not an answer I wanted to share.

"He wants to do an album."

"He's a musician?"

"Yes. In a rock band, actually."

"Then what does he want with you?" Linda gasped, slapping her hand over her mouth. "Oh, I'm so sorry! That sounded so rude."

I walked into the building, Linda trailing me.

"No, it's okay. I'm definitely not a rock kind of girl. That's why I turned him down."

Linda, her eyes still wide, cleared her throat as we walked down the white-walled hallway toward my classroom. "Lauryn. You didn't."

"That's not my life, Linda."

"Because you don't want it to be or because it's never been that before?" Linda asked.

Good. None of the parents or kids were here yet.

"I'm not much of a performer."

Linda raised her eyebrow. "You want to be boring?"

I smiled, but even I knew it was rueful. "I want to be *safe*. I'm so tired of feeling unfocused."

"Oh, sweetie." Linda draped her arm over my shoulder and squeezed. "Widowhood isn't for the faint of heart. I can only sort of imagine what you've gone through, and I know these past couple of years haven't been easy. But you must know you deserve to live. And live fully."

I tapped my key against the silver door knob. "I'm trying."

Linda smiled. "That's what matters. For now. Eventually, you'll get back into the full swing of life. So, what type of album does he want to do?"

I opened the classroom door, flicking on the lights. "Lullabies. For Valentine's Day. And as a wedding present to his brother and soon-to-be sister-in-law."

Linda made a soft sound. "That's so remarkably sweet. Like he needs more going for him than his looks and talent. Is he as nice as I'm imagining?"

I turned on the peppy, happy music the kids loved before removing my coat and hanging it on the hook. I opened my guitar case. I considered her question as I tuned my guitar. Linda sat next to me, waiting. I glanced up at her, my heart slamming against my ribs. "I think, maybe, he might be nicer."

Linda hummed, her lips turning up into a smile.

I picked out a little tune, my fingers too nervous to stay still. "I think I like him."

"I haven't met him, and I like him. So. What's the problem?" she asked.

I looked up into her tired, concerned eyes. She'd understand. She'd been my friend, helped me through those hard days when my husband left on his last tour and during that horrible period when the US Army brought his body home.

"What if he's what I want and not what I need?"

"Like Desden?"

I blew out a breath, trying to release the tension building in my chest. "Exactly."

CHAPTER FOUR
Jake

Getting around on the right side of a car was surprisingly intuitive. I liked the sporty hybrid SUV Murphy purchased a few weeks back. It zipped around corners but was substantial enough to feel like a real vehicle.

Yeah, driving in the States wasn't so bad, though I still wished I didn't need bodyguards with me wherever I went. The blokes were discreet. I barely noticed them outside Ryn's classroom or at the café. Good at blending in, a skill I was thankful for, especially when I walked Ryn back to her building earlier.

Alan and Isaac spoke little. Half the time, I forgot they were in the car with me. And today, they avoided my gaze, probably embarrassed by my second strike-out with the beautiful baby music teacher. No. Early-childhood music instructor. If I wanted to work with Ryn, and I did, then I needed to have the right mentality the next time we spoke.

I turned onto the expressway and headed east. I'd been itching to check out the Frye Art Museum, and I had a free afternoon, thanks to Ryn's brush off. Excitement buzzed through me as I paid for a ticket for Alan and Isaac and another for myself.

"I know this isn't your thing, mate."

Alan shrugged, arms crossed over his chest, but Isaac looked around, wide-eyed.

"I've never been in an art museum before, Mr. Etsam."

Poor as we were after my mum booted my dad, I'd managed pocket money from mowing lawns and cat- or dog-sitting. Because Mum spent all hours at work, Murphy was my constant companion—he taught me to surf, and I taught him the difference between a Reubens and Vermeer.

Now, that same thrill tingled through me as I explained the lush landscapes and cows painted in oils—pointing out Baer's distinct brush strokes before we moved into Gorter's delicate *Winter Landscape*. After an hour, Isaac's gaze started to glaze. He stepped back closer to Alan, no doubt ready to rest his overloaded brain.

I continued to stroll through the exhibit, content to study each painting at length. After another hour, possibly more, I settled in front of Ludwig Zumbusch's *Child with a Brown Tam O'Shanter*. A lovely image of a mischievous child, rounded red cheeks plumped in cherubic perfection—much like many of the kids in Ryn's music class.

I pulled out my sketchpad from the gray messenger bag I'd carried in and doodled at the top of the page.

I ached with remorse at my stupid words. She might well think I was a high-and-mighty rock god based on my pushy behavior—her brown eyes clouded with something that looked remarkably like lust after I kissed her cheek.

My doodle turned into a child similar to the one before me but with Ryn's laughing mouth, her soft chin. Determination to win Ryn over grew in my chest. I wanted this album, not just as a prezzie for Mila, who'd been through so much these past couple of years, but also for me—to prove I was a creative driver and my tastes were just as sophisticated, as nuanced, as Hayden's.

I flipped to a blank page in my sketch pad and glanced up long enough for Zumbusch's child to laugh back at me, no doubt enjoying my dumbassery with a woman I respected near as much as I found attractive. I leaned against the wooden bench, enjoying the quiet reverence of the space. I settled in, pencil held loose in my hand as my strokes lengthened across the page. How best to salvage my desire to work with Ryn?

She was the linchpin of the album—her original lullaby, "A Moonlit Serenade," added the emotional depth and richness I needed to bring the project to Hayden's level. Asher agreed.

Positive critical feedback on the EP would give me my own standing in the musical talent pool that made up Jackaroo. More importantly, though, it would provide the funds needed to set up my other dream: a gallery to showcase up-and-coming artists; a springboard to their first success.

I smiled at my drawing—Ryn holding her guitar, making a funny face at one of the children. Lionel, his name was. Cute kid with a good set of pipes. She brought that out of him, much as she made my heart beat faster each time she sang.

She wanted me near as much as I wanted her. With patience and perseverance, I'd win Ryn over. No matter how much effort I needed to exude, my gut told me Ryn was worth the time— professionally *and* emotionally.

I closed my sketch pad and stood. I'd just have to make the deal too sweet for her to pass up.

CHAPTER FIVE
Ryn

Dinner with Dez's family always left me nostalgic. I smiled as I pulled into the drive, thankful for all the memories that tumbled out and around me—not unlike the three of us when Dez, his twin sister Sam, and I were younger.

I walked into the house without knocking, just as I always did. But this time, for the first time in years, that action felt off. Like I didn't have the right.

Because of Jake?

He might be interested in me, but I'd brushed him off. Too bad I couldn't stop thinking of him.

"Ryn!" Joyce exclaimed, wrapping me in a tight hug that soothed me even as guilt flooded my chest. "We've missed you, honey." She pulled back, brushing my hair back and cupping my cheeks. "Aren't you pretty as a picture? Dez always did say you were the most beautiful girl to grace any room."

Her words hit my chest like a sledgehammer. I closed my eyes, unable to look longer into my mother-in-law's.

"I miss him," I whispered.

She hugged me again, tighter. "We all do, sweetie."

"Hey, Ryn. Good to see you," Sam said as she wandered into the room.

"Where's Ted?" I asked.

"Finishing up some paperwork. He said to tell you hello and he's sorry he missed you tonight."

I nodded as Sam slouched against the mantle that held a minishrine to Dez—pictures of us in our wedding finery, Dez, so young and handsome in his dress uniform. The flag that had wrapped his coffin leaned next to the photo Joyce took of Dez at his graduation ceremony. On the other side sat the last photo we knew of him—a quick snapshot from one of his buddy's phones. In it Dez, held his rifle, his eyes trained on some far-off threat that ended up killing him mere hours later.

"You girls hungry? We should eat before it gets cold."

I turned away from the memorial, more confused than I'd been when I walked in the door, and followed my mother-in-law and sister-in-law to the dining room table.

<hr />

Jake didn't call me that night. I'd expected him to, stressing about the possibility throughout dinner with my in-laws. Neither did he stop by the next day during classes—though I found myself listening for him.

After my three o'clock class, Linda brought me a large bouquet. My eyes widened as I asked, "What are those?"

"Looks like shakers and stickers."

My heart melted and pooled into my chest cavity as I touched the *PAW Patrol* stickers. Hundreds of them bound together into the "stems" to the flower-shaped plastic shakers. Jake had seen how much the kids enjoyed both the first time he came to my class.

"Man pays attention."

I nodded absently at Linda. "Was there a card?"

She handed it to me, a smug smile gracing her face.

I want to get to know you better.

Jake

I was in over my head. Already. In just three days the blasted man managed to irritate me more than anyone I'd ever met and, now, he'd managed to worm his way into my good graces.

I pulled one of the shakers out. It was bright red, bigger than the ones we normally used. The kids would adore them.

I bent over my phone. Taking a deep breath, I replied to his note with a text.

I love the bouquet. It's the best one I've ever received.

"Okay. I said thank you."

I slid my phone into my back pocket. Linda stood there, an expectant look on her face. It morphed into surprise when kids' voices slid down the hall toward my room.

"That's it?"

My phone pinged before I could respond. I pulled it out as the first of the kids slammed into the room, their voices bright with excitement when they saw the bouquet Linda settled on my bookshelf under the large window.

Glad you like it. You're doing amazing work with the children, and I wanted to help in some small way.

My hands shook as I stared at the screen. He was good. Shakers *and* compliments about my work. Dez said working with toddlers was a "cute way to pass the time." But Jake…a world-class musician, called it *amazing*.

I glanced to see the moms moving around the bouquet, smiling at its uniqueness.

"Who gave you these?" Calla, one of my longest-attending parents asked. "They're awesome!" She grabbed one of the butterfly shakers, her eyes alight with laughter as she danced around her four-year-old son.

"Her boyfriend," Linda answered as she sailed toward the door.

My phone pinged again as the moms exclaimed over the sweetness. I glared, willing my cheeks not to flush with pleasure and embarrassment.

Spend time with me. Get to know me. Please.

Before I could second guess myself or even think it through completely, my fingers typed out a message and hit "Send." *Dinner tonight? My place. 7:30.*

Oh no. I stared at the screen, horror creeping into my chest. What had I done?

His response popped up on the screen in an instant.

No place I'd rather be.

Oh. Oh, dear. My breath caught. Jake was dangerous. He was famous, sexy. I was neither of those and never desired to be. He'd hurt me. That was why I'd tried to brush him off that first meeting.

But now that I'd talked with him more, I yearned for another hour of his time. For a real kiss, where his lips fitted over mine.

From the brief contact, I knew, deep down, Jake Etsam had the capacity to own my body.

I bit my lip, ignoring my shaking hands and got down to the business of teaching class.

———◆———

Why had I suggested dinner? My tiny apartment wouldn't impress a man who made the kind of bank Jake Etsam did. And cook? I had to follow a recipe at least thirty times before I was confident enough to make it for someone else. Which meant I made basic food like roasted chicken.

Jake had traveled around the world. Even if he said he liked simple dishes, chicken was ridiculous to feed to a man who'd been served at Versailles. Yes, I googled him after the lips-to-cheek incident yesterday—only to stare at myriad pictures of the two of us together.

The one where he'd saved me from the speeding car was both the best and the worst. His hand was splayed across my lower back, snugging me close to his broad chest. My hand was high on his shoulder, almost slung around his neck—as if we were embracing. As if he *wanted* to kiss me. Which he had. On the cheek. A friendly gesture. Urbane even. But not sexual, like I'd been fantasizing about since he'd placed his lips against my over-heated skin.

I settled on my only other potential dinner recipe: pan-seared scallops. I'd yet to mess them up, and thanks to Pike Place Market, I knew the scallops were fresh. I also purchased a huge boule of rustic farm bread, high-quality olive oil, and the fixings for a green salad. While the meal was simple, the bottle of wine should dress it up nicely. I'd gnawed at my fingernails as I worried over Jake's alcohol of choice. I was terrible with mixed drinks—never learned to make one. Which left wine and beer. After an extended debate, I'd added a six pack of craft beer to my cart. Dez drank beer—Miller Lite was his preference. But Jake was older, more sophisticated than Dez. He struck me as a man who liked high quality even if he did go for simple.

He better. I'd blown my entire week's grocery budget on this one meal. After putting the groceries away, I scurried to my shower, still shivering from the cold December air that had riffled through my coat on the walk home. I needed to warm up and rinse baby drool off my body. Much as I liked holding the little ones—mainly so I could be wrapped up in their sweet baby smell—at the end of the day, I didn't end up as sweet to sniff as they were.

Granted, the trip to Pike Place had taken longer than usual because a reporter followed me through the stalls glittering with fairy lights and fragrant with the scents of the season—the fresh pine was my favorite. Unfortunately, I didn't savor the experience today, as I normally would, because the reporter continued to pepper me with questions about Jake.

"How long have you known Jake Etsam? When did you start dating? Do you have long-term plans? Are you in his brother's wedding?"

I'd made the mistake of glancing over at the young man as I said, "No comment."

Maybe he'd sensed weakness—or my newness to being questioned. Whichever, the questions came faster. "Why did you step in front of that car? Did Jake save you? What's it like to be a widow at twenty-four? Do you have any thoughts on the war? What do you think about the new military spending bill working its way through Congress?"

I tossed on a nice tunic and some leggings, my stomach knotted from the memory of the journalist's intensity. I pulled my comb through my unruly waves when someone knocked on my door. I despaired the person's timing. Jake should arrive in ten minutes, and my hair still dripped down my back, and I hadn't put on any makeup. I shouldn't have stayed late to help Linda work on her latest composition.

Taking a deep breath, I opened the door, freaking out about who would be on the other side. Please, not another reporter. My smile faltered. Jumping jelly jiggles. This was worse.

"Lauryn," Sam said.

"Hello." I sucked my lips back into my mouth, unwilling to say more after taking in the tightness of her expression and the angry defiance in her eyes.

"Why are you all over the Internet?"

"A slow day, obviously."

She slammed the door behind her. "Are you seeing *him*?"

I scooted back, a mistake, because she took the movement to pounce.

"What? You come to dinner last night and don't think to mention you're gallivanting around with some...some..."

"I'd be very careful about what you say right now." I kept my voice firm. "Jake is my friend."

"Looks like a shitton more than friendship with the way he's holding you on that sidewalk."

"Stop it. You don't get to come over here, shrieking like a banshee."

"Dez is barely dead! And you're now *dating—*"

"I'm aware of when Dez died. *I* was the one who got the knock on the door."

Samantha wilted, her face crumpling into tears. "You don't miss him at all?" she asked, her eyes filled with tears.

I ran my hand through my wet hair. "Yes, I miss him. I always will. But *he* asked for that deployment." That was Dez—ready for action, adventure. Ready to help others.

Leaving me behind.

I gripped the door frame at that revelation. *Dez left me*—he didn't have to go, not on the last deployment.

Sam rubbed her leaking nose on the back of her hand. With a shudder, I walked over and grabbed her a couple of tissues. She wadded them all up and swiped at her nose. Not much better.

"Why have you moved on so fast?"

"It's been over two years since Dez died. Almost three since he left me for that last tour." Wow. Anger simmered, hot, forming a hard knot in my chest. I'd never been angry with his choice before—devastated but never considering his actions selfish.

"You'd been together forever."

I crossed my arms over my chest. "Maybe that was part of the problem."

"What?"

I dropped my head back and rotated my neck, trying to ease the tension Sam's words and shrieking produced.

"I didn't make Dez volunteer for that deployment. He did that without asking me. I don't know what he was thinking. He didn't talk much after he came home from his second tour."

Sam swiped at her eyes. "Because you pressured him about kids?"

I dropped my chin to my chest and gave her a long side glare. "I met you and Dez when I was four years old. You both knew what my home life was like. You both knew I wanted children of my own long before we were through puberty."

Sam scoffed, but she couldn't refute my points. She'd known me the same number of years as her brother. That's the problem with twins—I was supposed to be Samantha's friend, but I'd always been more drawn to her brother.

"Are you planning to turn this rocker into your baby daddy?"

"Stop it, Sam." I slumped onto a barstool and dropped my head into my hands. "I can't handle the antagonism anymore. I just can't."

"Then you shouldn't have—"

"What? What exactly should I have done differently?" I snapped, patience gone.

Sam drew herself up, her mouth twisted in that ugly sneer that meant she planned to let me have it.

Another knock sounded on the door. I stood, drained. "That's Jake. We're having dinner to talk about a project." I enunciated the word.

"Think about how much *my* family loved you when your parents wouldn't."

I winced because Sam hit her mark.

"You can't throw away years of caring for a…a…rock star. Mom's never going to approve."

Right. That's why I hadn't brought Jake up last night during dinner with Joyce and Sam. I stopped right in front of her. Placing my hands on her shoulders, I tried not to feel the deep cut of rejection when Sam flinched back. I failed. "Dez made his decisions. He paid for them with his life. That's the reality *we* live in."

Samantha wrenched from my hands and opened the door. She threw a tearful glare at Jake before stalking down the hall.

Jake stood in the doorway, rocking back on his heels. He wore brown-framed rectangular glasses. *Gah!* I loved a man in glasses. Especially tall, broad men in gray button downs, sleeves rolled up

43

enough to show strong forearms. I stared at him staring at me.

Those flutters filled my belly. Maybe Sam was right. Jake was so far outside my league—his lifestyle so beyond my ability to comprehend—we couldn't possibly synchronize.

"You 'right?" His voice was soft, his concern palpable.

Good gravy, I was in trouble. Because, even with our differences, *I wanted him.*

"Truth?"

He nodded.

"No."

"Figured." He stepped back, easing into the hall. "I can come by another time."

I darted forward and gripped his wrist, ignoring the sensations searing up my arm, the flutters in my chest, seeping down into my belly. "Get in here. I have way too many scallops to cook for one person." My chin wobbled so I bit my lip, hard. "And... and...I don't want to be alone."

He stepped through the door and wrapped his arms around me, resting his chin on the top of my head. I huffed into his chest. My arms curled up his back, holding him tight.

"Bad day?"

"Not until Sam came over and told me I was being unfaithful to her brother. Oh, and to ask if you were going to be my baby daddy."

Jake's chest muscles stiffened, but he didn't drop his arms. "Er. I'm not really ready for that yet."

"What is it with men and not wanting any responsibility?" I wailed.

"I'm good with responsibility, but there's a difference between paying bills and changing nappies."

"But you wear glasses!" I jerked from his arms as I pointed at them, somehow both fuming and nearly in tears. What was *wrong* with me? I'd never been this tied up over a guy before. Ever. And I'd just met Jake.

"I lost my contacts," he said, dropping his eyes. "Fell out in the shower."

"Can you stop?" I placed my hand on my chest, over my racing heart. "I can't think of you naked. You wear glasses...but you don't like babies."

"Never planned on having any."

I stiffened, my eyes searching his—as my heart cracked at his casual words. A child—a family of my own—was my life goal. My dream since I was six. "What?"

"Ryn, I like *you* and all."

He rubbed his hands up and down the soft denim of his jeans so the material molded to his thighs. I swallowed hard and forced my eyes way, but not before a deep ache built in my middle.

"I know I'm the one who pushed to see you again, but right now? You're freaking me out."

Still, even as his eyes darted around and he stuttered through the last few words, he stepped forward to knead the tense muscles in my shoulders. I dropped my head to his chest and moaned when he hit a particularly sore spot.

"You're right. I'm a mess. Sam does that to me."

"I thought your—er, he'd been dead a while you said."

I nodded, my cheek wrinkling the soft linen of his shirt. "Twenty-seven months. Thanks for the hug."

"Looked like you needed a cuddle."

I laughed. "I did. Are you always such a teddy bear?"

He stepped back fast, his cheekbones brimming a dusky red. "Never offered my services before."

My heart squeezed at the look on his face, caught somewhere between mortification and consternation. "I meant it as a joke. I really appreciate the hug, Jake. And I'm sorry I went semipsycho on you there."

He dipped his head in acknowledgment, his gaze trailing across my high-ceilinged, industrial-style main room. The space wasn't huge—just cozy—and housed my newish, brown twill sofa and love seat, a red leather club chair, a four-seater dining table in a rich mocha I adored, and the functional kitchen with white cabinets. His eyes lingered on the exposed red bricks and the stainless-steel appliances. "Nice place."

"Suits me." I wrestled with my nervousness as I strolled toward the wall that held the kitchen, needing the space. "Want a drink? I bought beer and wine. It's white. Supposed to be good with scallops."

The concerned look began to fade from his eyes. "Wine, then. Thanks."

Pulling out the corkscrew I slid it and the bottle across the counter. "You mind opening? We'll drink bits of cork if I try to open the bottle."

"Sure." He picked up the corkscrew.

I pulled down two blown-glass wine glasses Linda gave me last year for my birthday and set them next to him.

"You have a thing for specs."

No. I had a thing for Jake in glasses. Totally different. More of his sensitivity showed through with the glasses. I stuck my head in the fridge, needing to cool my cheeks and collect my thoughts.

"Your day go well?" I called.

"Fine. Look, you don't have to make me dinner. And I didn't mean to embarrass you."

I pulled out the scallops, busied myself pulling them from their wrapping. "You didn't. I embarrassed myself."

"Ryn."

"I bought all these. See? Way more than I could ever eat."

"Are you going to ignore me?"

I gripped the edge of my countertop. "I'm talking to you right now."

He ran his hand across the back of his neck, knocking his glasses slightly askew.

I dropped my face into my hands and moaned. He slid the wine glass toward me so I picked it up and gulped. Setting it down, I forced my eyes back up to his. He waited, relaxed, seemingly patient.

"Can I be honest?" I asked.

"I'd hope you always are."

The laugh bubbled out. "I try to be. It's just…you make me nervous."

"I'm just a bloke, Ryn."

"We'll agree to disagree on that. But that's not why. I mean, I'm freaking out about your fame. A reporter followed me around today."

"Are you all right? He didn't harass you?"

He had, but I shook my head, not wanting to complain about the hounding journalist.

"I'll deal with it. No worries. Should have thought to after our picture yesterday. Fair dinkum."

Jake's lips pressed downward, and my cheeks burned once again but I kept my gaze steady on his.

"That's not what I'm freaking out about. I-I never dated so this…" I pointed at my chest then his. "Is new to me."

He set his wine on the counter as his frown deepened. "You were married."

I waved my hand, negating Jake's line of thought. "Dez was there. You know? My next-door neighbor. Everything was easy. Almost scripted."

Jake picked up his wine, his large hand cradling the bowl with a delicacy I envied. I wanted him to hold me like that. He waited for me to finish.

"I don't know how to act around you. What to say or do. How to tell you I'm interested in your project because then I'm worried you'll think I want to sleep with you, and I'm not sure I'm ready for that—for anything you might offer, really." I spread my hands out. "Working on an album, that's going to be life-altering for me. And pretty much everything in my life changed two years ago for the worse, so the idea of going through something like that again freaks me out." I picked up my glass and drained it.

Jake took the glass from my hand. Probably a good thing based on how much it was shaking. Rounding the counter, he cupped my cheeks in those big, calloused hands, tilting my head back to meet his eyes through those delectable brown frames.

"I like you, Ryn." He paused a long beat, studying my face. "I haven't said that to a woman in a long time."

My diaphragm stuttered.

"When I stopped in that first time, I knew I wanted to work with you. Now, after lunch, after seeing what you do, I'm compelled to get to know *you*. Maybe…maybe more. If you're ready." He paused again. His hands shook against my cheeks. "Can you live with that?"

"I-I…yes." My voice was breathy, so unlike me.

"As you make dinner, will you tell me more about you?"

"Yes."

"And—maybe—if we agree to it later, will you let me kiss you good night?"

My cheeks were so warm, they had to be burning Jake's palms. The heat crept down my neck, over my chest. "Yes." The word was barely audible. My stomach rolled as my thighs clenched. Jake, taking charge of the situation, made me burn.

He waited a beat while I tried to regulate my breathing. I didn't, and the ache between my legs grew.

"Is there anything else you'd like to add?"

My gaze dropped to his mouth, flicked back up to his eyes, which gleamed behind those sexy-as-sin frames. Dropped to his lips again. He held his breath, waiting to see what I'd do next. "Yes."

"What's that?" Now *his* voice was raspy. That meant desire, right? Before I could chicken out, I leaned up onto the balls of my feet and pressed my lips to his—just as I'd fantasized since he walked into my classroom a few days ago.

His lips were softer than I expected. Firm. I dragged my tongue across the bottom one, shocked by how different the texture was from my own. He gathered me closer, one hand sliding to my lower back and clasping my hip as if he couldn't stand any space between us. I settled against his chest, one of his thighs between mine, his lips still pressed to mine.

He dropped his hand farther and cupped my bottom, pressing me tighter to his thigh. He pulled back and hissed a curse. I continued to grip his shirt, unsteady on my feet, as I reached up and touched my lips. They were plump, slick. Tingling with need.

"I didn't expect that." His voice was rougher, his muscles taut—with need?

My limited experience with men frustrated me now. I wanted Jake to want me with the same desperation I wanted him, but I wasn't sure that was possible. Or plausible.

Releasing his shirt, I stepped back. "Me to kiss you?"

He stepped closer, caging me between the counter and his thick arms. "Yes."

"I—it's the glasses," I whispered.

He chuckled. "Well, if I'd known that, I would have started wearing them on stage."

My face crumpled at his words. I didn't want to think of other women kissing him, loving him. Oh, that hurt.

"Hey, come back."

I shook my head, embarrassment lighting my body up hotter than a blow torch.

"I didn't mean to…you scrambled my brains with that kiss. That was one of the hottest moments on my life."

I blinked up at him. "You thought that was hot?"

He pressed closer, his thighs bracketing me. "Yeah."

"Oh." My hands drifted from his hips, over his waist, sliding up, up to his chest. He was so muscular. I liked his size because he remained gentle, careful.

50

Fine. I liked Jake Etsam. A lot.

"May I kiss you again?"

I sucked in a shuddering breath before I managed to nod.

Liking Jake wouldn't end well. Which meant I'd just signed my own ticket for a broken heart.

CHAPTER SIX
Jake

This time, I claimed *her* mouth. My tongue slid across the seam of her lips and, when she opened for me, I plundered the sweet, warm heat with long strokes that got me hotter with each slick. When Ryn hummed her approval, I tilted my head and delved deeper. She sagged against me. I gathered her closer because I wasn't done with her yet.

I used my teeth. Tiny nips that had her making these little gaspy noises deep in her throat. My hand fisted in her hair at the base of her neck as I tipped her head back. Our tongues dueled and danced, and I craved more.

Her arms wound tighter around my neck as she flattened her delicious breasts against my chest. The kiss sped past passionate straight to wanton. The chemistry I'd sensed when I saved her from the car and then again when I kissed her cheek exploded into a haze of mind-numbing lust.

I pulled back in slow increments, needing to hold on to her. Bloody hell, this woman could kiss.

"We steamed all the windows," she said.

She sounded as dazed as I felt. I dipped my head against her damp hair, struggling to fill my lungs. Her scent swirled through me, making me ache for more.

"I've never done that before," she murmured.

I pulled back enough to stroke her hair away from her over-heated face. "Pash?"

At her look, I struggled to get my head straight. "Kiss. Make out, you Yanks say."

52

Her lips remained puffy and slightly parted, her eyes gleamed with desire. "Never 'pashed' enough to steam up windows." Her lips curved up in a small smirk. "Maybe it's just you. All those rock-star pheromones."

I snorted. "You're good for the ego."

"Glad to know I have uses."

"I'm coming to find you have many. Now, what can I do to help with tea?"

"Tea?"

"Dinner."

She nodded, disengaging with what seemed like reluctance from my embrace. I liked that—I could pretend she didn't want to let me go. I sure as hell didn't want to those soft curves out of my hands. As soon as she slipped away, I fisted my hands to keep from reaching for her again.

"Sit at the bar. I got this." I barely heard her mumble *I hope*. I turned away, not wanting her to see my smile.

I slid on to the barstool and swiveled back to face her once my lips returned to a neutral position. "You like it here?" Her view was stunning—Christmas trees sat in others' windows up and down the street, in a range of whites, reds, and silver. In the distance, Lake Union's placid water flashed with moonlight and, to the left, Christmas lights edged many of the masts in the marina. Her lobby doors were laden with pine wreaths and the fresh scent lingered in the lobby where Alan currently sat, no doubt glaring at every resident.

"My apartment or in Seattle?"

I wanted to know if this was the place she'd lived with her ex but wasn't sure how to ask. "Both, I guess. My brother loves

ALEXA PADGETT

Seattle's vibe. And Hayden's pretty settled, but that might be because Briar's family's all here. He doesn't have any now that his mum's passed on."

She dried her hands and pulled out a large cast iron skillet. "It's weird how casually you talk about people I've seen on magazine covers or heard on the radio."

Concern crept up my neck like tiny ant feet marching toward my skull. I shivered. "Is that a problem?"

She shook her head. "I don't think so." But the frown marring her brow deepened. She was as leery of the fame as I was—the journo pestering her today wouldn't help with that. I couldn't tell her that without sounding like a whinger. And I didn't know her well enough to tell her I'd never set out to be in a band let alone one of the biggest names in the business.

"To answer your question, I've always lived in Seattle. Went to Northern. I'm all of twenty minutes from the neighborhood where I grew up." She tucked the wayward strands of her hair back behind her ear and rubbed her hands over her long tunic. Her hair was mostly dry now, the soft waves from this afternoon fell down her back in a riot of curls. Her hair seemed to have a life of its own, rippling and spiraling about her head in a sexy cloud.

When I stopped focusing on her hair, I homed in on her nervousness. Or was it sadness?

"I've lived here for about a year. I like the space, but I know it's small."

If her husband died in Iraq two years ago, then he'd never lived here with her. I blew out a breath, relieved not to share a space with a dead man. The memories of him were more than enough.

54

"I didn't mean to make you feel bad."

She glanced up from where she was pouring oil into the large stainless steel pan. "You didn't." She sighed. "Not much. I had my reasons for staying near home."

She sealed her lips as a small frown marred her brow. Not good, whatever ran through her mind right then.

"It's just…you've traveled everywhere." Her eyes flicked up to meet mine. "That's pretty intimidating."

I scratched a spot behind my ear, unsettling my glasses. Her eyes darkened as they fell on my frames. The specs turned her on. Planned to wear them more often 'round her.

"I've been to heaps of airports and venues, which start looking the same after a while. But I've not experienced much of the culture of a place. Even the people who surround us are pretty constant."

She placed the scallops into the skillet. A nice sizzle filled the air. She dumped the greens from the bright turquoise colander into a big wooden bowl before squeezing two lemons into a container.

"You didn't get to see the Louvre or London Bridge or the Taj Mahal?"

"No to all three."

She flipped the scallops with a narrow spatula and added a liberal amount of garlic, butter and some lemon juice. She added olive oil to the rest of the lemon juice and drizzled it over the greens. Shutting off the burner, she moved the large skillet to the oven. After grinding a pretty pink salt and some fresh pepper to the greens, she tossed them with quick, efficient strokes of her wooden salad tongs. She pulled a large loaf of bread from the oven and started slicing it on the narrow butcher block island.

"You're scary with how economical you are in the kitchen."

"I like to cook. Just simple things."

She smiled, her cheeks deepening to a pretty rose. Probably because of my profession, but it was rare for me to see a woman in such a relaxed state. I loved how Ryn's hair rioted around her head, her cheeks flushed with natural color, her clothes simple and comfortable, her small feet bare. Her lashes weren't as long as many of the women I'd met, but I'd bet hers weren't enhanced.

I liked her like this. Natural. Easy. Lovely.

She handed me knives and forks, a couple of embroidered napkins. I laid the settings out and refilled our wine glasses. She brought me another set of glasses and a pitcher of water. I filled those glasses while she pulled down a couple of plates and added a large portion of salad and some scallops. She handed the plate to me.

My mouth watered and my stomach gurgled with appreciation. "This looks fantastic."

She walked to the stool next to me and slid onto it. Offering me the bread basket, she glanced down at her plate, her expression rueful. "It's one of the few things I can cook well, consistently."

"All you need is one dish to make it a signature." I raised my wine glass. "To a lovely dinner with an even lovelier companion." Ryn blushed again as she raised her glass.

I cut a scallop and popped it into my mouth, savoring the bite. "Definitely your signature dish."

"Thanks. Tell me more about this project."

"Lullabies. The whole album. Some traditional. Some new,

like the one you wrote. Asher's got one. I do, too. We're working on those now."

"And you want it out for Valentine's Day?"

I swallowed my bite and blotted my lips with my napkin. Mum would be proud of my manners. "Yep. It's a fast turn-around."

She raised her brows. "No kidding. You only have two months."

"We have about half the album completed. I reckon we're all right."

"I won't sing 'Rock-a-bye Baby,'" Ryn said, spearing at her lettuce.

"Why's that?"

"Have you listened to the lyrics? They're horrible."

"Then we scratch that one. We've already recorded 'Shenandoah' and 'Sleep, Baby, Sleep.' Now, your tune. 'A Moonlit Serenade.' Beautiful title. What made you think of that?"

She grabbed a piece of bread and sopped up the butter from her scallops. "Nope. Not sharing the reason for the name with you."

I settled back in my chair, holding my wine. It was local—I'd checked the label. Washington produced a great Chardonnay. "Fair enough."

She toyed with her fork, before setting it down on her half-finished plate. "How many songs?"

"Minimum of ten, preferably twelve if you'll sign on."

"A full-length album? In two months?"

She'd fixated on the timeframe, which made me nervous. "Right-o. We're not writing much for this. Using old standards. Asher's finished 'Shenandoah.' He said his mum used to sing him that one. Preslee Jennings is in the studio next week and the week after if we need her."

"That's quite a lineup. You don't need me."

"I want you." I rubbed my hand on the back of my neck. "Came out a bit wrong. I mean, I do want you. As a woman. But that's not what I was talking about just now." Blimey. My cheeks heated and those ants marched down my spine. I sent this convo to shit awful fast.

Ryn leaned over and placed her finger on my lips. I stilled, hardly breathing. Her touch exploded magical heat inside me. Like fireworks to my guts. No wonder I craved this woman so much.

"Can I think about it? I mean…it's just well…recording albums, hanging out with rock stars…that's not something I ever imagined in my life."

I cupped her hand in my larger one, pressed a kiss to her palm. "Could be. Easy as."

Her eyes held anguish and something darker. Guilt or some other self-destructive emotion. "I'm not trying to be a pain. I promise. But…like you said, I sing songs for babies." Her voice turned tremulous, and I'd bet a lot of her hesitancy revolved around the woman here when I showed up. Sam. Her sister-in-law.

"You do much more than sing. I've heard you, seen how the kids connect with you."

She smiled a little, pride pushing her chest out. "You were there maybe fifteen minutes."

I leaned in, making sure her gaze locked on to mine so she could see the honesty there. "And you blew me away."

She dropped her head and shook it. Right-o. Time to back off. For now. "My mum sang 'Sleep, Baby, Sleep' to Murphy and me. I recorded that one first. Do you have a favorite? From childhood, I mean."

She hesitated before shaking her head. Strange. Ryn sang lullabies for a living. She had to have a favorite.

But then, she'd never mentioned her parents—just Dez's—in our conversation at lunch. I cleared my throat, unsure how to get us back on better, safer ground.

"I want us to do a duet. Asher has the better voice, but this is for Mila and Murphy first and foremost, and it's about the only thing I can give them they can't get themselves."

She picked up her wineglass and took a sip, staring at me over the rim. "Why a duet with me?"

"Because your tune gives me chills each time I listen to it. When I played it for Murph, he went near ballistic when I told him he couldn't sign on to the project. That's how good your voice is. It'll carry mine."

She blinked at me before her entire face flamed bright.

"I think that's the nicest compliment I've ever received."

We ate in silence for a bit and I enjoyed the meal she'd made me. But I needed to ask the other detail that nagged me.

"So why would someone want to mow you down?"

Her fork clattered to her half-empty plate as she gaped. After she managed to close her mouth, she asked, "What are you talking about?"

"That car. It aimed right for you."

"No way." She shook her head, hard. "There's no way."

"I was there and saw it happen. The light had been red for ages. It only shot through when you stepped off the curb."

"But…why? Who?"

I resettled my glasses on my nose and peered at her through the lenses. "Dunno. You can't think of anyone who'd want to hurt you?"

Ryn picked up her fork but it was just to push the food around her plate. "Besides Stephani? No."

"Who's Stephani?"

"And that's why she wants to hurt me," Ryn said. Her chuckle was forced, but I appreciated the attempt at humor. "The girl who asked you out in my classroom. Young. Blonde. Curvy." Her brows rose with each of the final three words until they all but disappeared in her hairline.

"Oh, right. The sheila who got sicked on by the nipper. Yeah, she was a right nuisance. But with a bub in the car?"

"It was a red car, right? Stephanie drives a little red Audi."

"Didn't catch the make. The windows were tinted dark, but I know the plate had a K and a 6. We should check out her car when she comes in next week."

She shook her head, anxiety flashing in her eyes. "I'm not sure it's her. Steph is just young. She's not mean-spirited."

I let Ryn have the last word because I planned to find out what Stephani's license plate was before the next class. "Can you think of anyone else?"

Ryn licked her lips, but this wasn't in invitation. Her eyes darted left then right, landing anywhere but on me.

"Ryn?"

"Sam," she whispered.

My chest ached as if it hollowed out with that one syllable. "The woman who was here earlier?"

Ryn smoothed her long, wild curls, the shadow of pain building in her eyes, sliding across her skin. She'd paled too much. "Dez—my husband—she's his twin sister. Her name's

Sam. Samantha."

"Of the baby-daddy shaming comment?"

Ryn nodded. She tugged at her tunic, balling the material into a tight knot at her hip so a thin slice of her pale stomach showed above her leggings. If the situation were different, I would've loved the slow strip tease.

"She's not happy with me," Ryn said. Her voice wavered.

I reached for her, not willing to chance a fall. The skin on her arms was chilled. I pulled her closer, unsurprised by her shivers.

With an easy lift of my arms, I helped Ryn settle into my lap. She nestled in tighter, needing the connection as she considered the possibility I brought up. Bloody hell. Should have kept my mouth shut.

But then Ryn might be in danger. Remembering the trajectory of the car; the sharp whine of its engine and the direction of the front end as it flew closer to her, I knew Ryn *was* in danger.

"What kind of car does Sam drive?"

She sucked in a deep breath. Then deeper. The words came out a rasp, nearly as painful to hear as to speak.

"A red Honda Civic."

CHAPTER SEVEN
Ryn

"You can't think it was her, though." My words sounded defiant—not strong or sure. I fisted my hand on my thigh, thankful for Jake's proximity even as his question made me want to pace around the room.

"I bloody can and will," Jake said, his voice sharper than usual. "Most people know their attackers. Mila's was her step uncle."

I tugged at my hair, trying to settle my nerves. "One, we don't know it was intentional. Two, who told you it's someone you know? Are you sure that's true?"

Jake's intense gaze drilled into mine. "Yes, I'm sure." He paused, sucking in his lower lip, almost as if he wished he'd stopped talking long before he had. "Someone ran that light—directing the car at you. Taking that lightly, blowing it off, opens you to danger. And…" He looked chagrined. "And it's possible the person was a fan. Some feral with a mad crush."

"On you?" I asked, amused. "You think someone tried to kill me so they could get with you?"

Jake grimaced. "I didn't say that. But situations like that have happened before."

"To you?"

He flapped his arms in exasperation. "No."

I laughed, thankful for the release of tension that had built in my shoulders and neck. Jake scowled harder.

"Look," I offered, patting his biceps. "If something else happens, I'll call the police."

He glowered, but I didn't back down. No way Sam wanted

to hurt me. And if it was some random fan…well, it wasn't like Jake and I were together. He was wooing me to be on his album. No need to worry about kissing him because that wouldn't happen again.

Finally, Jake sighed. "That's going to have to be all right. But I still register protest. And I'm going to suggest you look at Sam's license plate. If it has a K and a six, you bloody well better call the police."

I shivered, trying to force away the concern Jake's word built within my chest. "Noted. And I promise."

I slid from Jake's lap, and he stood. He tugged me forward and wrapped his other arm around my waist. He bent his head toward mine. "I'm going to kiss you. Then you're going to tell me to leave."

"I am?" I asked, surprised and turned on all at once. And with one look from those hazel eyes, I'd already relinquished my promise not to kiss Jake again. My lips tingled in anticipation—a sensation I relished. "Why?"

"Because I'm not going to want to stop with just a few kisses. And we've just met. You and I both need to consider what a relationship means to us."

"We're in a relationship?" I asked. He didn't really want me—did he? No, he wanted me to work on the album, not build a life with me. Pssh, I needed to get a grip. Just because Dez settled into a committed relationship with me didn't mean Jake wanted—or planned—to do so. And…and…I hadn't dated anyone since Dez. Hadn't wanted to. Sam's visit tonight made me realize she and Dez's family weren't ready for me to start a romance. Not that Jake planned to romance me.

"I want us to be. But, as you said, you've not dated much, and I don't want to ruin my chance by coming on too strong. But just so you know, I plan to call you tomorrow. To set up another date."

Joy spread through me at his words. He wanted to see me again. In a romantic setting—not a business one. Our attraction rocked me, but maybe Jake always created fireworks in the women he kissed.

I swallowed down the lump building in my throat and forced a smile. "Are you always this methodical?"

"Yep. Drives Murph troppo."

The unfamiliar word caused my growing panic to subside. "Troppo?"

"Crazy. He says he can't stand my plodding approach to life."

Jake said he wanted to kiss me. I wanted that, too. Very much. Turning him away now would be stupid—something I'd regret for ages. I sucked in a breath and tried to act much braver, and sexier, than my thoughts allowed. "Well, I'd prefer you kissed me rather than told me what comes next."

"That I can do."

He covered my lips with his, and I pressed up toward him, needing to feel his chest against my breasts and his tongue in my mouth. His slow slide of lips drove me crazy, and I gripped the back of his neck as I angled my head. Jake's muffled moan sent throbs of awareness into my lower belly. I slid my tongue over his lips before nibbling at his bottom one, pulling it into my mouth.

CHAPTER EIGHT
Jake

Care to give away some gifts tonight? I asked Ryn via text. *What did you have in mind?*

I smiled. I liked her speedy response, her up-for-anything attitude. *Mila talked Murph into going to the Mercer Island Tree Lighting. If you want to go, we can tag along.*

You're inviting me to meet your brother at a Christmas event?

I rubbed the back of my neck, trying to ignore the building tension there. *Thought it would be fun. Festive. Cold. We don't do cold Christmases. Mila's desperate to meet you. Please?*

My phone pinged with her response nearly an hour later, and the entire time, I worried I'd overstepped somehow. What if Ryn hated Christmas? Or didn't celebrate it? Or…my mind spun in way too many directions, and I struggled to make the calls and send out the necessary e-mails to keep my lullaby album moving forward.

Asher's e-mail with Preslee's studio times this week had my heart plummeting further. I'd signed on everyone I wanted except Ryn—the linchpin of my project, and she wouldn't bloody text me back about a date tonight, let alone answer me about singing.

Just what I deserved for wanting to start a relationship with someone I was desperate to work with.

Sorry—was on a phone call. Okay, but only because I want to give little kids presents. I've never done that before.

I heaved a sigh of relief—good, she wasn't avoiding me.

I'll make Murphy sing your favorite carol. I replied.

Really? That would be amazing! Though…is it a big deal that

I'm half Jewish? I mean, I grew up celebrating both Hanukkah and Christmas.

Ah. See, that's what came of assuming Ryn's background was the same as mine. I'd made her uncomfortable. I set my phone down and rubbed my palms across my face. Served me right.

I needed to hear her voice, reassure her and myself that I wanted this date.

I pressed her number and ignored the crazy trip in my breath as I brought the phone to my ear. *You're a rock star, Jakey. Talking to a sheila you like is easy as.*

Biggest lie of the year.

"Hello?"

Hearing her voice, my jaw loosened and the words flowed. "You got to celebrate both Hanukkah *and* Christmas? You won the jackpot on holidays."

She made a strangled noise somewhere between a laugh and exasperation. "I was confused for years. I didn't understand why so many people didn't do it the same way as my family. My parents weren't all that demonstrative." Her hesitation made me think they were even less demonstrative than she let on. "I went to Christmas activities with Dez and Sam and their parents, but my mom insisted I go to synagogue every Saturday for years."

"Do you prefer one set of traditions now that you're an adult?"

"I—I don't know." Her voice suggested a story there. "I mean, they're important to me for different reasons."

"Right-o. Which is why we go to the tree-lighting thing tonight and then some menorah-lighting thing another night."

I pressed the phone tighter to my ear, praying I'd gotten Ryn's vibe—and the details of Hanukkah right. I felt like a bloody damn fool with my face all red and my heart hammering like a bass drum.

"I'd like that."

Her quiet words, filled with both uncertainty and pleasure, caused me to fist pump. Good thing I was alone in my hotel room.

"I'll pick you up at six."

"I'm looking forward to seeing you." Again, her voice was hesitant, but I loved the words spilling past her lips.

I clicked off, rested my phone against my chin. Not half as much as I look forward to seeing her.

Because of Mila's shoulder—and Murphy's overprotectiveness— Ryn and I offered to take the wrapped toys over to the donation site. Now, after eating and drinking too much, we wandered back toward the place Murphy texted he and Mila were.

Children in hats and coats, some with half-off scarves trailing behind, shrieked past the towering tree of red poinsettias. Blue-topped tents held a variety of food-stuffs, hot cocoa, and information about the night's events. A line of candy canes and lit spiral trees led to the stage where Murphy and Mila waited. Ryn smiled at it all, her mitten-clad hands clasped together in excitement. The mittens made me smile—a soft gray yarn with bits of red and white mixed in. Festive but not overt.

"I've never come out here for the holidays before. This is fun." Another passel of kids—probably ten—raced past us.

"Usually I'm in shorts and sunnies for this holiday. Seems odd to bundle up." I rubbed my hands together to warm them up.

Ryn stopped walking and stared at me with big eyes.

"Our Santa surfs into town."

"Must have been strange, watching American Christmas movies."

I laughed. "Considering we rarely saw snow, yeah."

"We're not much for snow. Just cold."

She shivered as the brisk wind riffled through our clothing.

"You sure you had enough to eat? Once Murphy plays, we'll need to head out. Or be mobbed." I scowled, disliking this aspect of fame more than my other bandmates. No more casually taking my girl out for an evening together; this required security and a bloody schedule, no matter how impromptu I'd made it appear for Ryn.

She patted her belly, which was covered in three or four layers of clothing. "I'm stuffed."

I wrapped my arm around her shoulder. "Thanks for coming with me."

"Thank you for inviting me. I'm having a great time."

She grinned up at me, her eyes clear and full of happiness. I liked seeing her like this—I wanted to ensure she always did. I'd begun to realize my feelings for Ryn had developed before I even saw her—I'd fallen in love with her voice. But then I met her. I liked her, I wanted to spend time with her.

Kissing Ryn…I hummed in the back of my throat. Best experience in years. Maybe ever.

She stiffened as a man with a camera popped in front of us on the path, snapping away. Alan moved in from my left side and spoke to the photographer, who nodded and trotted off.

"Sorry 'bout that. Shouldn't happen again."

She nodded, eyes wary as her brows pulled low. I held my breath, wondering if she'd ask to leave.

"Dropping off the gifts was fun." She beamed up at me, letting the bad mood float off on the chilly wind. "Did you see the kids' faces?"

"Better than your hot chocolate?" I teased. The Northwest might be health conscious, but that must fly out the window this near the holidays. Her hot chocolate was more like a tub than a cuppa, topped with a massive pile of whipped cream. Ryn put it away like a champ.

She practically bounced up and down. "Yes. Though the cocoa was fabulous."

"Then we'll find another place to donate some stuff."

She stopped walking, so I stopped as well. Her mouth slid into a flat line or seriousness.

"You don't need to do that. I don't want you to think I expect you to do that."

Confusion settled over me. "I offered."

She blew out a breath. "I'm weirded out by your world. The photographer...you think nothing of dropping hundreds of dollars on kids' toys, but for most people, that's a huge budgetary sacrifice."

I wrapped my arm around her waist, needing her closer to me. "I'll make you a deal."

When she tilted her head back and raised her brow, all that long hair spilled over my arm. She appeared feminine but not in a fussy way.

"You do this album with me, and I'll let you buy the next round of toys."

She laughed shaking her head. "That's *two* things that benefit you."

I leaned in, unable to resist the opportunity to taste her happiness. The kiss bloomed into passion much too quickly for a public locale. Reluctantly pulling away from her, I said, "How about you do the album, kiss me like that later, and I'll buy the next round of gifts? Hanukkah ones."

"You're wearing me down."

"With my generosity?" I asked, pulling her tighter to my chest once more. Exactly where I wanted her, journos be damned.

She hummed in agreement. "And your thoughtfulness."

"That's it?"

"And your kissing skills."

Not what I needed to hear whilst standing in the middle of a park, though her words warmed my insides. I took her mitten-clad hand back in mine and squeezed. "Better. Good recovery there. Let's go find Murphy and Mila."

We walked to where Murphy was standing, cuddling Mila, in the shadows of the stage, well behind the glare of the lights. He wore a thick black parka like the people here seemed to prefer and a black knit beanie and gloves. Mila glowed in her pristine white knee-length coat. I smirked, wondering if the color choices were intentional.

"Jake!" Mila's face lit up when she saw me, and Ryn stiffened next to me. "You get the prezzies delivered?"

"Yep. No worries."

"I thought you said she's like a sister," Ryn muttered.

Oh. Wow. That sounded like…was she jealous?

Far as I knew, no woman had ever been jealous over me. I'd

seen multiple catfights over Murphy, hell, all my bandmates. But women never fought over me.

Murphy stepped forward and held out his hand to Ryn before I responded.

"Pleasure to meet you, Ryn. Heard your voice. Bloody marvelous."

Mila laughed, smacking his arm. "He's toning down his language for you." She leaned in closer to Ryn and put her arms around her. Ryn's arms circled Mila, careful of her shoulder wound. "I'm thrilled to meet you! Jake's chatted about you nonstop. Plus, I love your lullaby. The bub and I listen each day during my physio. Helps me work through it." Mila grimaced.

"I'm so glad you like the song." Ryn smiled, but it was cautious, maybe a little unsure. "Jake's told me about you, too. I'm so sorry you were shot."

"Wouldn't want to do it again," Mila said. "But it did get rid of my stalker and give me back Murphy." The look she shot him glowed with love; Murphy, unable to resist the temptation, pressed a kiss to her lips. "Made it worth it."

"No, it fucking well didn't," Murphy growled, his brows pulled low and dangerous over his nose. "But you're a'right, and so's our bub."

"I am. And now you're going to sing me my favorite Christmas carol while I stand here and get to know Ryn better. Life's heaps good, Murphy. Let the rest go."

Murphy continued to grumble, as he always did. Seemed to think he could get in the last word, which Mila allowed as it assuaged his pride. Ryn's stiffness faded as we stood there, probably the ridiculousness of my brother so in love loosening her fears. Whatever the reason, I was glad she'd relaxed back into my side.

"I like this," I murmured into the knit cap covering her head. "You, here, with me, spending time with my family."

She shot me a look I couldn't decipher.

"I'm on," Murphy said. This time, he pulled Ryn into a hug. "Might not get a cuddle after. We're off to visit Mum next week so be sure to stop by before," he said to Jake.

Murphy turned his stern gaze to Mila. "You stay close to Claude and do not, under any circumstance move. Or I will quit singing to paddle your bum."

Mila rolled her eyes and she inched closer to the large man, who'd stood behind us, arms folded across his chest. "Here I am. Next to Claude."

Murphy leaned in and kissed her long enough for me to feel bashful.

Murphy whispered something in Mila's ear, causing her to smile and blush. He nicked the mic from the stand and settled his guitar strap before bounding up onto the stage, yelling, "Happy Christmas, Mercer Island! Glad to be with you in my new home."

The crowd roared, as it always did when Murphy took the stage. Ryn watched him, awe growing in her eyes, as he worked the audience.

"It's his super power," Mila said with a sigh. "He loves the attention, and they do lavish it on him."

He strummed his guitar and began to sing. The rest of us stood, rapt, as he performed. He segued into a second song, then a third, and I smiled, pleased to see Murphy giving this mini concert for no other reason than the sheer joy of it.

When he finished, he leaned in closer to the mic. "I have a surprise for you, Mercer Island. One of my favorite female singers is here, just waiting to sing you my favorite carol."

I stiffened, but it was nothing compared to the tenseness radiating from Ryn. Mila's face lost its smile. She touched Ryn's arm.

"He didn't tell me. I would've told him not to."

"He doesn't mean me," Ryn said, voice faint.

"You know why it's my favorite?" Murphy winked. "Because she's singing it."

The crowd hooted and howled. Small children screamed and clapped. Probably the best tree lighting concert they'd ever have.

"Join me, Ryn Hudson. The folks here need some more Christmas spirit."

Ryn turned to me, wide-eyed. Murphy boxed her in, and I wasn't happy about it. And by the pulse beating in her throat, she wasn't either.

"I don't perform in front of crowds," she whispered, her voice as desperate as her eyes.

Murphy beckoned her up, beaming like he'd just handed her a huge cash check. The areswipe! I might just bloody his face for this.

"It'll be all right," I said, keeping my voice soothing. "It's just like performing for your babies. You're so good with them."

"Because they're babies! And they don't care, really."

The crowd began to grow impatient, craning to see who Murphy was waving to. The smile slid from his face as he caught a glimpse of mine, then Mila's. Ryn's was buried in my chest, as she shuddered through another breath.

"I'll come up with you. You can do this."

She tipped her head back and met my eyes. "What if I suck?"

I smiled as I swiped her cheek with the pad of my thumb. "You won't because you can't. That voice of yours is mesmerizing."

She sucked in a breath and nodded. "Okay. But don't leave me."

I turned her toward the stage and clasped her hand. "Promise."

She climbed the steps to the stage, her hand gripping mine. The crowd clapped politely but they already shifted, unsure of the newcomer who took too long to respond. My heart rose into my throat. The crowd needed to accept her, love her, like they had Murphy.

"Whatcha gonna sing for us, love?" Murphy asked.

She looked out over the audience, gauging their reaction to her. "Well, I didn't really have anything planned."

Murphy raised his eyebrow, as if his douchery finally settling over him. "Jake here says you like 'Jingle Bells.'" Murphy smiled for the crowd, who hadn't heard Ryn's response, but this time his grin was strained.

Ryn also apprised the crowd. She took a deep breath and let go of my hand. She removed her mitten and held out her hand for the mic. Murphy handed it to her as trepidation built in his eyes. If Ryn bombed, Mila and I would ream his arse.

Before any of us could say anything, Ryn started singing. Those first few notes were midrange but powerful. "The First Noel…" As she continued to sing, Ryn closed her eyes and let the lyrics take her. I'd heard multiple stars sing this song. None gave me goosebumps like Ryn had when she hit the pure, high note in "Israel."

The woman *sang*. And she did it without any accompaniment,

without earplugs. Her talent overwhelmed me, and I stood as enraptured as the crowd as she finished the second verse.

She lowered the mic from her mouth and glanced back at me, where I stood in the shadows. "How was that?" she asked.

I stepped forward and wrapped my arm around her shoulder, pulling her close enough to whisper in her ear, "Amazing."

She smiled and did a small wave before handing the microphone back to Murphy.

Murphy grinned and bowed.

She turned to leave, but the crowd booed, then began chanting, "More, more!"

I hissed out a breath, thankful and a bit overwhelmed by their reaction.

"How about one more song?" Murphy asked, wiggling his eyebrows. His piercing caught and flashed in the lights. "Give us a mo' to confer. We've not sung together before."

He turned off the mic and walked over to us. His face morphed onto the pained look I knew well. "I'm a bloody arse."

"I don't really like to sing for crowds."

"Why not?" Murphy's surprise built. "Bloody fucking Christ! With pipes like those, I'd sing my way through life. And make some fine quid doing so."

"She doesn't, and that's all that matters," I growled, stepping closer to my brother.

Murphy met my gaze, his features austere in the lights. "Got it. Won't happen again." He blew out a breath. "Any song we all know so the crowd doesn't riot?"

"'Jingle Bells,'" Ryn and I said in unison. I grinned down at her, excited that we were already sync—excited to share my love of music with her.

Murphy turned on and raised the mic. "We need two more microphones and a stand," he said, buying us a few more seconds. He dropped the mic back to his side.

I smiled down at Ryn. "We can ask the kids to sing, which the parents will like."

"Smart, mate," Murphy said. "But I haven't played that one in years. A bit rusty on the chords."

"I'll play it," Ryn said. "That is if you don't mind me taking your instrument."

"No worries." Murphy handed it to her, and she took off her other glove, shoving it into her left pocket. Once the microphones were in place, we turned toward the audience, almost in perfect synchronization, and smiled.

"We've got a classic for ya," Murphy crowed. The crowd hollered.

Ryn strummed the notes and all movement in the audience stopped. "All right, boys. Let's jingle some bells."

Murphy and I joined her, letting Ryn's guitar chords set the pace. I went to stand next to her while Murphy hammed it up with the crowd.

"Remember how I did it with the kids?" she asked.

I nodded.

"Okay, that's how we're playing this audience."

She began to play and Murphy stepped back, letting her own the limelight. Once again, Ryn's voice was killer—precise yet meltingly sweet. Murphy kept time on his thigh, joining in for the chorus. I added some deeper bass as Ryn worked her way up to harmonize with Murphy. He grinned at her as she met him note for note. By the last verse, we *owned* the song. The crowd clapped and sang along. This was one of the best highs I'd ever gotten while performing.

"Your turn!" Murphy called to the crowd. "Jingle Bells…"

Their voices filled the cold night air, the festive mood building with each note.

"Fair dinkum!" Murphy yelled when it ended. "What did I tell ya? Ryn Hudson, everyone."

We took our bows and headed off the stage. As the crowd surged forward, no doubt wanting our autographs, Claude and the rest of the security team stepped in front of us, a human line just behind the metal barricade.

Mila latched on to Murphy's arm and from the set of her lips, I doubted Murphy would like her next comments. He hung his head and nodded as Mila led him away.

"You ready to be off?" I asked.

"She does have him in hand, huh?" Ryn said, her gaze lingering on Murphy and Mila, who was still giving him an earful.

"I'll make sure he apologizes for putting you on the spot like that."

Ryn laughed, and I realized she was still on the high from a great performance. "It's fine. Mila's dealing with him, and I had fun. Lots of it."

I brushed her hair back and pulled out her mittens from her pockets, holding them up so she could slide her reddened fingers back inside. "I'm glad."

"Ryn!" The voice was female, urgent. We both turned to see the sheila from her flat. Sam, Ryn had said. Her dead husband's twin. Not bloody likely this would go well.

Sam plowed forward, chest heaving and cheeks stained with tears. "What were you thinking? You never perform for crowds!"

"I didn't plan to, Sam. Murphy blindsided me. If he'd asked, I would've said no."

"Please." Sam's voice dripped with scorn. "Clearly the limelight suits you." She looked me over, her face crumpling. "Why are you here—with *him?*" Sam pointed at me. "What about Dez?"

I stepped closer, already concerned with Sam's tone and aggression. Sam glared at me.

"This is all your fault! Ryn can sing—whoopedeedoo! So can millions of other women. Go after one of them, but leave my brother's wife alone!"

I glanced around, mindful of our audience. Good thing Mila whisked Murphy away—he wouldn't handle this type of attack on Ryn well.

"Stop it, Sam." Ryn's voice shook with fury and, blimey, I hoped not, sadness. "Dez is *dead*. He's not coming back. Not to me, not to you." She sucked in a deep breath, her face taking on a fragile quality I didn't like. "And I deserve to have fun."

"I hate you," Sam spat. "If Dez could see you now, all cozied up to a—a sex-loving rocker, he would, too."

"That's enough," I snapped, unwilling to let this woman batter Ryn further. I lowered my voice as I dipped my head toward the security detail moving toward us. "You don't know me, and I resent your implications. You don't deserve to hold Ryn's happiness or tie it back to her dead husband. Now, these men, here, will see you to your car."

"I would have handled her." Ryn's voice sounded hollow. "I

78

needed to. It's my fight."

Oh, bloody hell. I'd stepped in the dogshite now. I might want to protect Ryn, but I hadn't earned the right.

"I'm sorry," I managed to stutter.

"Being an only child, I can't imagine how Sam must have felt when her twin brother chose me in kindergarten as his confidant and best friend."

"That's what happened?"

She nodded. "There was never anyone else."

Such simple words that explained much about her relationship with her deceased husband—and with his family. I'd mull that over more later. Now, I needed to do damage control. Not just for my mistake—but for Murphy's.

But her gaze flitted to the avid interest on the faces of those close enough to have heard some, if not all, of our interaction. My stomach soured as horror crept across Ryn's expression, taking in the cell phones pointed her way, probably recording this moment.

Yeah, this was when public life destroyed people's sanity. I'd dragged Ryn here, into my fame, blithely assuming all would work out 'right because I wanted her, us, so badly.

Without another word, Ryn gripped my hand and pulled me toward the back of the stage, where we'd parked a couple of hours earlier. Her hand trembled but her stride remained confident, her head up.

Blimey. She took my breath. Handled the would-be gossips and detractors like the champ she was.

Made me want her more—and made the ache in my chest and balls sharpen.

Once I settled her into my car, she wrapped her arms around her middle.

"I'm so sorry," she whispered. "I didn't know she'd be there. She doesn't live on the island."

"Not a thing for me." I started the car. "Dealt with worse. But seems like she's opposed to you seeing me." *And you're none too happy with me for stepping in.*

Ryn's face, pale and set, turned toward me. "Not her choice. I need to work out the details with Sam." She pulled off her mittens and rubbed her palms along her jeans-clad legs. "Dez used to protect me from Sam, too, but now..." She trailed off, a deep frown building across her brow.

"You still miss him, don't you?" I asked.

Ryn dropped her gaze to her lap and didn't answer.

I pulled 'round the lot, heading toward the exit. I saw Sam slide into the Honda Ryn had mentioned. I didn't catch the license plate because Sam pulled out multiple cars in front of me, but Ryn's white face and large, bruised eyes recalled our previous conversation where I all but accused her sister-in-law of attacking her.

Bloody hell.

So much for a cheery, merry night.

CHAPTER NINE
Ryn

Videos hit YouTube and media sites. Many of them were of me singing. Those I could handle. The one of Sam yelling at me—and the angry comments about me being a traitor to my husband and a cheat—those I could not.

After the twenty-third phone call from a variety of media outlets, I'd turned off my phone and tried to catch up on errands. I needed to stay busy and focus on something, anything, other than the painful spiral of my former life. I'd get out of my apartment and finish my holiday shopping. I sighed, pleased with the plan.

I'd stepped outside and another group of paparazzi tried to mob me.

Isaac, the larger of Jake's two bodyguards, had strode in front of me and crossed his arms, silently daring any of the collected journalists to shove a microphone into my face. None did.

"Thank you," I'd whispered to him.

He glanced back at me, the hint of a smile turning up his lips, brown eyes softening. "Thank Jake. He's worried about you."

I'd nodded, turned on my heel, and headed back to my apartment. More like my jail—that left me with my memories and an inability to quash the array of emotions rolling through me.

Jake and Sam were right—I did miss Dez, but not for the reasons Jake thought. Yes, I'd always love Dez because he was my first...well, everything.

He'd handed me a crumpled handful of tulips from his mother's front garden when we were nine—my first flowers from a boy. He'd kissed me at our eighth-grade graduation ceremony—my first kiss. He'd held my hand as he taught me to ice skate and then to Rollerblade, still two of my favorite pastimes. I helped him pick out his first apartment—that became *our* first apartment—weeks before the start of my sophomore year of college.

Dez was also the first man to break my heart.

I shouldn't have asked Jake to drop me off on Saturday.

Whatever Jake and I were building intensified each time I was with him. I'd told myself the space, the return to routine, would do us both good. Give us a breather, a chance to step back and think.

But now I was stuck in my apartment. I was so desperate for human interaction Sunday midmorning, I called my parents.

"Hi, Mom. I…"

"Yes, Lauryn? Did you *need* something from us?"

My throat dried. *Do you need something, Lauryn?* Your time, your interest. Possibly a little affection.

Mom huffed. "Your father and I were out the door to brunch with the Simmons."

I'd never met the Simmons or the Putmans or any of the other couples my parents referenced—not because I hadn't offered to visit, but because they were *too busy.*

"I wanted to see if you'd like to come spend the end of Hanukkah, maybe Christmas with me."

My mother sighed. "We've been over this, Lauryn. Your father and I raised you. You're an adult. Now, you need to live your life and we deserve to live ours."

I blinked back the tears that threatened each time my mother said something like this to me. The last time I saw my parents was at Dez's funeral. They left right after the service with barely a word of condolence.

"I met someone," I said.

"Good. That's good. You're young and need to share your life with a nice man. Now, if that's all, we're late."

The ache in my throat spread to my chest, causing my head to pound. "Bye, Mom."

She'd already hung up.

Isaac hadn't been outside my door or in the lobby when I left for my classes at seven thirty Monday morning, and I sighed with relief.

The media attention freaked me out. Peoples' comments hurt my feelings. But having a body guard? That was in a different galaxy than my world.

A world Jake slammed into and shook so hard I still couldn't get my footing.

I stopped just short of my classroom, my heart jumping in my chest.

The door was ajar.

I'd locked it Friday after my last class. I remembered turning the key, jiggling the handle to double check.

Reaching out, I pushed the door open with the tips of my fingers. A sob caught before it ripped its way up my chest and out my mouth.

Pieces of wood littered the room. The strings were still attached to the head, shooting out in various directions like live electrical wires. The fretboard was broken into three chunks, the body smashed beyond recognition.

My keys slid from my numb fingers.

"Hey, Ryn! I'd ask how your weekend went, but I saw you

splashed all over the papers with that sexy Aussie rocker. You could have told me you were going to sing at the Mercer Island event! I would have loved to hear you live. Though the recording was amazing." Linda walked up to me waggling her eyebrows. The smile slipped from her lips as she looked past me into the room. "Oh. My. God. What happened here?"

"I-I don't know."

Linda pulled her cell phone from her purse, juggling the bag, a to-go coffee cup, her brief case, and her violin. "Don't touch anything."

"What are you doing?" I asked.

"Calling the police. This is a crime scene."

My stomach lurched and the numbness from my fingers crept up my arms, into my chest. A crime scene. Smashing my guitar was intended to hurt me. Maybe send a message—of what?

Linda spoke into her phone, her tone clipped. She thrust her violin case at me, and I clutched it to my chest, unable to do more than gape and shiver.

"Come on." Linda tugged at my free hand, her voice gentler now that she'd dropped her phone back into her large, purple tote. "We'll get some coffee and wait for the police. I told them we'd be in my office."

"But. My class?" My voice ended on a higher note. Like it was a question.

"I'll talk to the secretary. We'll sort something out. My first concern is you. Then the kids."

I shook my head, anger burning off the numbness. "No. The families are first. I can't just cancel. That's not fair to them."

"We'll work something out, Ryn. Sit down."

In her office, Linda pushed me into the visitor chair in front of her desk. With a mournful look, she passed me the to-go cup she was holding. "Here."

"No. It's yours. I can't just take your coffee."

"Pfft. Drink it."

I put the plastic lid to my lips and pulled a big gulp of peppermint mocha into my mouth. My favorite part of the Christmas season, right here, in a cup. My vocal cords sang with approval. Swallowing, I took another mouthful. "Oh, that's good," I moaned.

"Shut it. I only allow myself one of those." Her eyes followed the cup.

"Why? This is true love for my taste buds."

"I know," Linda said with a sigh. "But there's, like, a million calories per sip. It's worse than cheesecake."

"How can coffee have more calories than a slice of cheese-cake?" I asked, frowning at the white lid.

"Not a *slice*. The whole damn thing. Or near enough. Feel a little more capable?"

I nodded. "I can't believe someone did that to my guitar."

Linda shook her head. "That was more than straight up vandalism. That was rage." She cocked her head. "Which I don't get. You're the nicest person I know."

I set the cup on the edge of her desk, needing a moment to compose myself. "I don't think it's about my job," I said quietly. "Something to do with me seeing Jake Etsam, maybe."

Linda clucked. "That man does exude sexy. I can understand some jealousy." Her brows pinched together. "But breaking in and destroying your classroom? That's a felony offense. Seems like more than what the typical fan would do no matter how much she—or he—wanted Jake for herself. Himself. Whatever."

I nodded, lacing my trembling hands together in my lap.

"I don't think it's a fan."

After catching the K and six in Sam's license plate, I was sure of it. That was a big part of why I sprinted from Jake's car when he dropped me off and avoided all calls and texts from the world yesterday.

I needed a plan, but I didn't have the first clue how to handle this situation.

"Finish the coffee. It's teasing me," Linda said, eyeing the cup longingly. "Who could it be if not a fan?"

Picking up the cup, the warmth from the cardboard seeped into my hands. I downed most of the beverage in one gulp. My stomach gurgled and my eyes teared from the heat, but I sighed, my taste buds blossoming with happiness, souring only when I opened my mouth to tell Linda my fears.

That's what I needed to do—confide in someone, get another opinion.

A knock at the door made me jump. Linda raised her brow and called out a terse, "Come in."

A uniformed officer pushed open the door, his face pale and beginning to sag. Creases faded out from the corners of his eyes and his jawline wobbled, the skin loosened by age. I closed my eyes, unable to believe the trajectory of my life.

"Ms. Kelly?"

"It's Dr. Kelly. Thanks for coming."

"Sure. Right." He stepped into the room. "You had a complaint, Dr. Kelly?"

"She does," Linda said, pointing to me.

The officer dropped his gaze to me. A slow smile spread across his face. "Howdy-do, Ryn. Haven't seen you in ages. Joyce's wondering when you'd be by."

"Hi, Ted." I stood and embraced my father-in-law. "I've been busy."

Ted patted my back in the gentle way of his. I inhaled his Old Spice aftershave and the starch Joyce insisted on in each of his uniforms. He'd smelled the same all the years I'd known him.

"Saw your picture in the paper this weekend, which had Joyce calling Sam. She didn't take it too good that you're seeing a new man." His eyes remained steady, the disappointment clear.

"Why is it your business to decide what makes Ryn happy?" Linda snapped.

Ted broke eye contact with me, leaving my legs shaky, to gaze at Linda. After thirty-three years in law enforcement, he had that deadpan face down. Unfortunately, he used it on the wrong person—Linda never backed down.

"Linda, this is my father-in-law. Ted, Linda."

Linda dipped her head, not bothering to rise from her chair to shake his hand. Irritation dripped from her eyes, settled into the curl of her mouth.

"I'm so glad you know Ryn. You can understand, doubly, how upset she is when you go see her classroom. The one someone trashed this weekend along with destroying a very expensive musical instrument."

Ted's lips compressed. "Your guitar?" he asked. "The one Dez gave you when you graduated?"

Ted understood how much that instrument meant to me. The

guitar Dez had bought before he left was the only legacy of my dead husband I'd ever have. Joyce snatched the flag they'd laid over his coffin when they helped me move last year, adding to the shrine of the boy-barely-turned-man who'd left me alone not long after he promised to always be there for me.

Not that I was bitter.

Fine. I lived bitter. Partly because I missed being married as much as I missed Dez. I looked away, not wanting Ted to read the shock and relief building with these thoughts.

When had I gotten to this point? *How* had I begun to think of my relationship with Dez in such a way? Guilt ate at my stomach, turning the once-delicious coffee sour.

"Aw, hell, honey. I'm sorry."

He patted my shoulder as his face screwed up, agitation mottling his dusky skin. His next words slid through my mind before he even spoke them. "Joyce isn't going to take this well. Not at all."

Linda's chair scraped back against the tiled floor. "I'd think you'd be more concerned about *Ryn*, considering that was her *beloved*, most prized instrument. The one she's taught with every day for the last four years." Linda's voice was sharp, the irritation clear. "Why don't you go have a look so that Ryn can start assessing the damage and figure out how she's going to teach today."

Ted shuffled back, his slack jaw surprising me. Sure, dealing with Linda was like that—a complete whirlwind of opinion and sass—but Ted was married to Joyce, who wasn't known for her easy-going personality. *High-maintenance* better described my mother-in-law.

"You mind going back in there, Lauryn?" Ted asked.

My shoulders clenched and my stomach twisted, but I answered as Ted expected. "I'll be fine."

"You always have been a tough girl." Ted patted my shoulder. "Much tougher than my own. Appreciate the lack of tears, you know."

I wasn't sure I did. In fact, crying seemed like a damn fine idea right now.

I led him back down the hall to my classroom where another man now stood.

"Isaac?" I murmured.

"Didn't get to your place early enough to escort you, Ms. Hudson. Jake'll ream my as—er, rear for that." His dark skin reddened.

"I'm not your responsibility."

He raised a brow. "Yes, you are. Jake said so."

I sighed, not willing to fight with Isaac—not while Ted looked on, avid interest burning in his eyes.

After introducing the two men, I moved to the doorway of my classroom again.

My stomach plummeted when I looked at the damage once more. Such a waste. Like so much that had happened these past few years, I couldn't wrap my mind around the senseless destruction.

"Well, I'll be." Ted rubbed his index finger over his lip—a gesture he made when he was contemplating a theory. "They didn't even try to take the little stereo."

"Dock," I said. At his blank look, I explained, "The stereo portion is a dock. It's worth a few hundred dollars."

"Why didn't the thieves take any of that?"

Annoyance flashed quick and hot through my veins, leaving my hands shaking and my voice cold. "I don't know. But trashing my guitar wasn't just a senseless act of violence. It was premeditated. Look at the bits of wood—whoever did this smashed it many times. And ripped the kids' scarves, cut the floor mats." I sucked in a great gulp of air, trying to calm my frantic heart rate, ease the ache in my throat. "This was vicious."

Isaac stepped back, pulling his phone from his pocket. He turned away from me and spoke into it softly.

Ted scratched the back of his neck, near his collar. "Mmm."

I gritted my teeth. After two deep breaths, I turned to face him, showing Ted my shaking hands and letting the tears that had threatened earlier fill my eyes. "Anyone who knows me knows I loved that guitar, that I love my job. This"—I gestured to the room—"was to hurt me."

"She wouldn't, you know." Ted's voice was almost a whisper.

My body shook with the building anger. "Oh, Sam *would*. We both know she loved Dez more than anything. And she's already told me twice that I shouldn't be dating." I wrapped my arms around my waist and stared at the tiny pieces that had once been a beautiful sheet of highly polished wood. "She always blamed me for him leaving. She told me again on Friday and yelled at me on Saturday. That's online if you don't believe me. Half the world's commented on how I'm a bad person because Sam's tirade made it sound like I'm still married."

I took a deep breath, left my arms wrapped around my middle and met my father-in-law's eyes. I'd promised Jake if something else happened, I'd talk to law enforcement.

"And she drives a red sedan like the one that nearly mowed me down last week. She threatened me at my house and then screamed at me after the Mercer Island tree lighting. Now this. She's escalating, and I'm scared."

———◆———

The first class of the day passed in bouts of melancholy and myriad temper tantrums and tears. Toddlers liked routine. Moving to a different room without the brightly colored floor and the extensive variety of plastic instruments frustrated all the children. I spent the five minutes I had left before class started herding the parents and children to the temporary music room and searching for a guitar without success.

More than the changed room, my lack of a guitar—the one I let them crawl over and strum—left the children downright angry. One little girl broke out in tears when I started clapping the "Hello Song" and didn't stop until her nanny, completely frazzled, gathered her up about halfway through the class. By the end, I had a massive headache and even more tension building in my shoulders.

"Sorry about today," Ginny said. She grappled with her screaming two-year-old, deftly dodging his kicking feet. "Ugh. Boots were not a good choice. We'll talk about the change some more. Now that Dylan knows, he'll do better next time."

"Next week we'll be back in my normal room. I'll pick up a new guitar as soon as I can. I'm so sorry I didn't have one for the kids today. I'll see about a makeup class."

"That's nice. Especially since the kids all acted like little monsters."

"Change isn't fun. I get that." Boy, did I. I blew out a breath, but it did nothing to ease the pressure in my skull.

A hand settled on the back of my neck and began to rub. I moaned, closing my eyes.

"Omigod. Don't stop. That feels so good."

"Looks like." Jake chuckled as he turned me to face him, his hand continuing to knead my neck. "And from the tension I'm feeling here, you need some relief."

"I'll owe you forever if you can give me that," I said. "I'm prepping for a killer headache."

"Anything, eh?" Jake continued to press his fingers into the sore spot and I hummed with pleasure, my head dropping forward and onto his chest.

I popped open an eye. "Within reason."

"Will you stop avoiding me?"

I sighed. He would realize that's what I was doing. "Yes. I'm sorry."

"Good. I want to take you to lunch. My shout."

"You don't need to do that."

"Fair dinkum, Ryn. You've had a morning of it. Least I can do is buy you a meal. It'll offset the dinner you made me."

"That wasn't a problem. And I enjoyed eating with you."

Jake leaned in, his nose brushing my hair. "I brought you a guitar."

I stared at him, mouth agape. His cheeks reddened and he cleared his throat, but thank goodness he didn't stop rubbing my neck.

"Isaac called me." He hesitated, but added, "And I saw on

the news." His smile held sadness. "Since your name is linked to mine, that makes you newsworthy. The reporter mentioned the break-in, the destruction of your instrument. I know how much the kids liked it…"

I threw my arms around his neck, trying hard not to sniffle into his dark Henley as I squeezed him tight. "Thank you. So much."

He returned the squeeze, his hands sliding up and down my rib cage. "My mum tells stories about Murphy. How much he hated any type of change."

I pulled back, needing to look in his eyes when I said, "This was the nicest thing you could have done for me. And I-I'm sorry I shut down on Saturday. Yes, I'd love to go to lunch after my next class."

He rubbed the back of his neck, mouth flattening into a line.

"What's wrong?" I asked.

"Would you—is it okay if I stick around?"

I narrowed my eyes, trying to figure out what he was up to. "Why?"

Jake Etsam wanted to hang out, here, in my class room. He'd been here before, but I'd been annoyed by his interruption. Now, it was like he expected me to teach him something. As if that was possible.

"You're a talented musician, Ryn." His eyes narrowed to a squint. "Murphy agrees with me."

"What?" My voice squeaked. Holy sweet potatoes. This week was filled with crazy. And it was only ten thirty on Monday morning.

"Right-o. Anyway, he suggested I bring his guitar."

I pointed a shaking finger at the case. "That's Ets's guitar?" I whispered, unable to force more sound out of my vocal cords.

"One of them. The one you played on Friday."

Luck. A. Duck. Jake Etsam wanted to watch me do a children's early music program without any preparation. With his brother's expensive guitar. I couldn't swallow past the lump building in my throat.

"You can say no," Jake stuttered, his voice a little shaky. Like he was nervous. Why would he be nervous? The flutters in my tummy were a roiling mass, and my neck cramped in a long, vicious clench.

"No I can't. But, jeez, Jake, give a girl a chance to prepare. You're famous. Like, really."

His grin bloomed across his mouth, lighting up his whole face. "Nah. Not really."

"Shut it. I can't take the joking right now."

"No teasing, then." He set the guitar case to the side and pulled me back into his arms—almost as though he couldn't stop touching me. "I won't bother you."

I thumped my head against his chest twice. "I'm not worried about you bothering me. I'm worried about how bad I'll mess up. How much the moms and other caregivers will rip me apart when they come in to find a superstar hanging in the room and they haven't put on makeup or even clean clothes."

"That happens?"

I snorted. "Ask your brother after his baby's born."

"Why the hell would you give up on personal hygiene?"

"You don't give it up. You choose sleep and eating over showers and clean clothes. You know, priorities."

Jake's eyes widened as he once again homed in on the tensed

muscles in my neck. "A tiny baby is that disruptive?"

A deep belly laugh escaped from my lips. Jake frowned in response, perplexed.

I rolled my eyes. "Okay. You win."

"I win what? You've confused me."

"You can observe my class. And you're cute when you're confused. And babies are a ton of work, and these women deserve to have that work appreciated."

"Blimey. I thought I won you singing on my album. But I'm glad to spend time with you."

When he said things like that to me, I melted. "I…" Not ready to go there. "I talked to Ted. He's a police officer and Dez's dad. He came by, took my statement about my classroom, the guitar." I inhaled deeply. "I told him what we knew about the near hit-and-run, too."

Jake's fingers hit the biggest knot in my muscles and my eyes crossed as I sighed with pleasure. "Ahh. Your fingers are magic."

"I'll rub your neck for a bit longer. Until you decide I'm worth the risk." His fingers pressed harder into the knot.

I lifted my head and met his worried gaze. "What's wrong?"

A million expressions danced across his face before he finally blurted out, "I'm worried you're going to tell me to go away."

"Why would I do that?"

"Because—"

"Ryn! Is it true you spent Saturday night with…" Susan stopped talking as I lifted my head from Jake's chest. "Oh my… Oh my…"

"Hi, Susan. Sorry we had to change rooms this morning. Mine's a crime scene."

Susan's mouth opened and shut, her eyes large and unblinking. "You're…you're…"

"This is Jake," I said, hoping to stave off any kind of shrieking. My head couldn't take the noise. I rolled up onto my toes and whispered in Jake's ear, "You might want to give me ten minutes? That'll give me time to prep my class."

Jake pressed his thumbs into the still-tight muscles in my neck one more time, and I moaned. "You can't make noises like that," Jake whispered back. "I like them too much."

I raised an eyebrow, and he sighed.

"I'm going to the art building. Be back in fifteen minutes, maybe a little longer."

He pressed his lips to my cheek and I whimpered, unable to resist the urge to turn my head and press my lips to his. Jake stepped back when Susan made a strange, strangled noise.

"See you in a mo'," he murmured back. He dipped his head in greeting to Susan, who looked just like a shocked cartoon character, and walked out the door.

"That's…Jake Etsam….You kissed…."

"He's going to observe the class today."

Susan practically collapsed to the floor, but in true mom form, she clasped the head of her infant strapped into the carrier on her chest. "You can't do this to me, Ryn!" she shrieked. "I didn't sleep more than three hours last night, and I threw on my oldest pair of yoga pants. They make my butt look flat."

"I didn't know he was coming by," I said. "He brought me a guitar because someone broke mine." Such an understatement, but I didn't know how to explain the rage that created the splinters of my once-beautiful instrument.

96

"Okay," Susan said, her voice soft, her eyes closed. "Okay." She opened her eyes and glared at me, raising her finger to jab it in my direction. "You invite him back sometime when we all look nice. That means at least a full day's notice. I want a selfie to post on social media. You make that happen or I'm telling everyone I know how awful your classes are."

"Roger that," I said with a salute. But my attempt at humor hid a deeper, more pressing worry. I needed this job—not just to pay my bills but because this was the closest I'd be to a baby of my own.

I swallowed down the bitterness and anxiety of my life, trying to push back against the dread of knowing I'd never be a mother, and knelt and opened the guitar case, my hand shaking as I wrapped it around the gleaming wood. This guitar made my Taylor look like a cheap toy.

I ran my hand over the instrument, marveling at the smooth curves. The rosewood gleamed.

"Get a new guitar? That's pretty," Jan said from the doorway. "Why are we down here?"

I explained the situation as the other seven moms streamed into the room. They all gasped in sympathy at my destroyed instrument and bemoaned their lack of makeup and decent clothes when they found out who was joining the class. One mom frantically finger-combed her hair before the woman beside her handed over a hair tie. Both looked close to tears.

I started the "Hello Song" about three minutes before the class started because I couldn't handle the tension.

Murphy's guitar played like a dream with beautiful sound and receptive nylon strings. I'd been missing out—driving a Cadillac instead of a Rolls Royce. Now that I'd played an instrument of this quality, I wasn't sure I could ever go back. The children, aged five months to four years, had no clue why their mothers weren't interested in class today, because they were rocking out to my version of "If You're Happy and You Know It."

I placed the guitar carefully in its case as I segued into the kids' favorite: "Here is the Beehive" and the children made buzzing sounds. Those old enough rolled around on the floor, too.

The door cracked open and Jake poked his head through the doorway. He tiptoed in as I began an energetic rendition of "Wheels on the Bus." The kids loved the swishing wipers.

By now the adults had noticed our guest, but I ignored my shaking hands and asked Owen, my oldest student, what he'd like to sing next. He chose "This Little Light of Mine" because we added the shaker instruments—his favorite activity—to the song. I passed those out—the extras I kept inside the locked closet down the hall, not in my room—as I took surreptitious breaths.

Owen and Luka sang the lyrics with me, along with Sonia and Mae, twins who weren't quite three. When they hit the right pitch, I grinned at them, gesturing with my hands for them to increase their volume. They bellowed the third verse, all on key.

"Great job, everyone!" I said, clapping. The girls squealed and tackled me.

"We did it! We thang the whole thong!" Sonia said. She bounced up and down while her sister squealed.

"You did. I'm proud of you."

"Again!" Luka said.

"All right," I averred, not wanting a temper tantrum to mar

Jake's classroom experience. "But then we have to put away the shaky eggs."

Mae poked out her lower lip, a sure sign she wasn't happy. Her mother, Jeanne, a woman in her early forties who'd taken off this year from her high-powered partner position in a prestigious law firm, said, "I bet if you ask Ryn, she'll sing 'Shenandoah' while you put away your instruments."

My stomach twisted and fell, but I managed to smile. That song was difficult to sing, but I managed to get through our second rendition of "This Little Light of Mine" and "Ba Ba Black Sheep"—another child's request before I had to sing the lullaby alone.

I set the instrument basket in the middle of the floor and reopened the guitar case. I settled the strap around my neck, my gaze darting to Jake, who leaned back against the wall, arms crossed and eyes narrowed. I gulped as I strummed the chords. Closing my eyes, I focused on the first lyrics. The lullaby had long been one of my favorites, so I was comfortable with the sliding notes. I opened my eyes and smiled as I continued through the second verse, glad to see all the children were cuddled into their caregivers' arms.

I finished the song, letting my voice faded out. The kids sighed. Before I could stop myself, I glanced back up at Jake, whose eyes shone with appreciation.

"You want to help with the last couple songs?" I asked.

Jake's smile widened as he walked around the circle to plop down next to me. "My favorite song is 'Kookaburra,'" he said. "You know that one?" he turned toward the children, who nodded. The adults were back to fidgeting and gawping.

I plucked out the opening chords and let Jake start the song, adding a soft soprano harmony to his baritone. The kids stood and started to bounce to the tune while the women in the circle stared, eyes wide.

We finished with a flourish and Jake wrapped my shoulders in a hug. "That was fun. Do we have time for another?"

"Of course! If you name a kids' song, I can play it. But, this is your brother's guitar. Why don't you play, and we'll sing?" I tried to hand him the guitar but he shook his head.

"Nope. If you know it, you'll do it better justice for the nippers." He smiled around the room, and the mom's sighs were filled with longing.

I strummed out the chords to "You are my Sunshine" and the kids popped back up. I smiled as the older boys made suns with their small arms, their palms barely touching over their heads. This time, all the kids and most of the moms joined in for a beautiful rendition.

At Jake's request, I played my lullaby before the "Goodbye Song," knowing how much the kids needed the transitional reminder. Many of the babies were drowsy, their eyes drifting closed. Susan slid her daughter back into her sling and stood. "Remember your promise, Ryn," she said, her face stern. Then she turned to Jake and smiled. "Thanks for the songs. This was awesome."

The other moms nodded. "I took a video," Jeanne said, her cheeks turning a lovely shade of pink. I'd never seen her look sheepish. "I wanted to show my husband that he's wrong about the importance of music. And…" Her cheeks flamed. "To show my colleagues at work that mommy time can be exciting, too."

"Right-o," Jake said, probably because he was about to be an uncle. "You show 'em how we rocked it today."

Jeanne's smile widened, her pretty eyes brightening. "Thanks! I'll send it to Ryn so she can post it and tag the other moms."

After they clamored for autographs, the room emptied.

"Are you okay with that?" I asked them, rubbing my damp palms against my jeans-clad hips.

"With our picture on your website or whatever?" Jake asked. "Reckon." He shrugged. "Might be good for business, yeah?"

Did he think I'd use him for publicity?

Before I could ask, Jake said, "I'm impressed."

"Murphy wants to bring Mila next time. He said they've got to get their nipper into lessons soon as. If you ask him, he'll want his face on your promotional materials, else he'll get his feelings all crushed."

"I…" No more words came out of my mouth. What had happened to my life—and in less than a week?

Jake rocked back on his heels. "You're on lunch, right?"

I nodded through my daze.

"Then let's take you out for some tucker."

CHAPTER TEN
Jake

Murphy texted me before I went into Ryn's class, and after I told him I was meeting Ryn for lunch, he invited himself.

I cringed through the entire hour and a half, thanks to Murphy's stories about his and my antics growing up. Ryn chortled at many of my less-than-stellar moments, especially the time I caught a blue-ringed octopus in a sand bucket and begged my mother to keep it.

"So, there's Mum, trying to remain calm and explain to Jake that the octopus was poisonous, when he reached into the bucket to pet it. Mum slapped the bucket out of his hand better than any footy player stripping the ball."

Ryn picked up her napkin, dabbing her eyes and holding her belly.

"Jake started screaming about his hand stinging and Mum thought the octopus bit him, so she's calling for a lifeguard, sobbing her baby's been bit." Murphy picked up his seltzer water and sucked on the straw.

"You love to tell this story, wanker."

Ryn scooted closer so she could lay her hand on my chest. "It's pretty funny. But you weren't stung, were you?"

Murphy snorted. "They bite. And no, not even. He was whingeing from Mum's slap. Once we figured that out, boy was golden."

Jake continued to look nonplussed. "Don't know as to all that. Mum wouldn't let me go to the beach until I pointed out every dangerous animal there and could recite their deadly facts.

Morbid, if you ask me. And took me the rest of the summer. Didn't get to go back till the following year."

"Served you well on your report in grade eight," Murphy shot back. "But you were always studious. Followed the rules, this one."

"Would've rather been surfing," Jake said with a shrug. "Just wasn't one for making Mum upset.

The two of them turned quiet, introspective. Whatever the reason, their love for their mother shone through on their faces and in the way they spoke of her.

"What about you, Ryn?" Murphy asked, turning toward her. "You have any stories to share?"

She shook her head, cheeks turning a pretty pink. "I was a quiet kid. I liked to play house."

Murphy leaned back against the booth, throwing his arm over the top. "Like Jake, then. He was quiet and baked with Mum. Me? I played doctor, not house." His grin broadened. "Mila *is* a doctor, which makes my exams that much better."

Ryn's blush intensified, and I wrapped my hand over the top of hers. "None of that, Murph. And don't think I haven't noticed you didn't apologize properly—the only reason I let you tag along."

Murphy's ears turned red and he played with one of his piercings. "Jake's right. Don't much like to say I'm wrong, but I was. I shouldn't have assumed that because I like to perform, you would too. I put you in a bad spot."

She reached over, laying her hand atop of his where they were clasped on the table. "Thank you for that. Really." She patted him twice. "Just...could you maybe remember to ask me first next time? I do better when I'm prepared."

Murphy shook his head, his dark hair and piercings adding

a dangerous edge that covered his kind heart. Mila's return to his life meant a reemergence of the thoughtful bloke I'd grown up with. I ticked off another day until their wedding—looking forward to Murphy tying the knot and settling in to his role as husband and father.

He'd be much better at it than our father.

I never planned to have kids. Not since I learned in one of my grade ten courses that poor parenting could be a genetic trait.

No way a child of mine would ever be subjected to a bad influence and total jerk-off like my father had been.

"I need to get back. Thanks for coming by today. Oh! I need to give you your guitar!"

Murphy waved Ryn off. "No worries. Keep it. The bubs like it, and I have a few more."

"I couldn't. It's too much," she gasped.

Murphy placed his forearms on the table and leaned forward. "I hear you haven't answered Jake about his project. Consider this a signing bonus."

Ryn's eyes were wide as she glanced back and forth between us. I held still, breath baited for her reply.

"I'll speak to your brother about the album, but I'd feel better if—"

Murphy's phone rang, his newest—and best-selling—tune titled "Hold You Close." He whipped it out along with his wallet. He dropped some bills on the table and slid out of the booth as he spoke into the phone.

"All right, Mila. Just finishing up here with Jake and Ryn." He stepped away from the table, ignoring everyone and everything as he strode toward the door where one of the bodyguards stood.

"Did you have a guard with you the first day we met?" she asked me, gathering her purse.

"Yep. Stood in the hallway outside, looking like hoodlums. Followed us to and from the restaurant, too. Alan helped me pull you back that day in the road. Can't be too safe—as we know since the car and the guitar incidents." I paused, eyes narrowed on her. "I'd like you to keep Isaac 'round. That'll put a crimp in your sister-in-law's threats."

I took her hand, pulling her from the booth.

"No need. Ted will see to Sam. But thank you for the offer."

I held open the door, and we stepped out into a light Seattle drizzle as I debated whether or not to force the issue. I tugged up the hood of my North Face jacket and Ryn slid on her mittens.

We hustled toward my car, and I opened Ryn's door before hurrying to the driver's side. I slid onto my seat and turned on the heaters.

"Where's Murphy?" she asked.

"Went back with the guards."

She pulled off her mittens and tugged at imaginary lint caught on one of the fingertips.

"Where's your guard? Alan, right?"

"Yep. Texted him I planned to drop you at work and to meet me back at the hotel."

"You and I don't live in the same world." She sighed, and I tensed. "Isaac's nice and all, but it's…weird, having someone following me around."

"You get used to it." I said because I didn't know what else to say.

"Do you?"

She was right. I hadn't. Didn't like the constant presence. Didn't like that mobs of fans attacked us wherever we went.

I scowled, wishing I'd met Ryn when I was just a bloke—a poor art student. Somehow, I knew that would have made her more open to me wooing her. My scowl deepened as I realized Ryn was married when I was in uni. Married and wanting babies. I bit back a curse. Murph might make a hella good dad, but that didn't mean I would. Or should try.

"Are you upset with me? That I won't just sign on to your album?"

I glanced over at her as I slowed for the stoplight, taking in her damp skin and the moisture clinging to her lashes. I loved looking at her. Her blond hair with shades from platinum to a rich honey—my favorite sweetener—shone even in the watery luster. Her light brown eyes glowed with sincerity.

"No. I'd never be angry with you about that. Disappointed, sure. Heaps. But I'm not sure I could ever be angry with you."

"I-I want to. Work with you." She dropped her gaze to her clasped hands. "I've never wanted something like this before. Before you strolled into my classroom, I'd say I was content with my lot. I love to teach."

"Now you've had a taste for performing live. That's why you weren't angrier with Murphy. It's a rush like no other."

"Better than I thought it'd be. But I like what I do. Most days, I love it. Can't imagine doing something else."

Ryn thrived around infants. She was made for mothering. I'd seen enough for that knowledge to seep into my bones. And Ryn...she was the marrying kind. Her first husband knew that and married her whilst she was still a teen.

Maybe dropping the *us* before we became a couple would save us both later heartache.

If that was true, why did my chest hurt to consider that move? Still, I needed to be honest.

"You love spending time with bubs and…I'm not ready for a baby. Don't know if I ever will be."

"Where did this come from?"

"Murph and I were remembering our dad at lunch."

"When you got so quiet."

"He beat the shit out of my mum till she miscarried my baby brother."

No. She mouthed the word, like her vocal cords were frozen with the shock.

I squeezed the steering wheel so hard, my fingertips numbed. "I can't lie to you. I don't want that between us. But if it's a deal breaker, I get it." I dropped my head back between my shoulders and my hands to my lap. "You have no idea how much that rat bastard broke us. I look just like him, Mum says," I thought to add. If his features sat on my face, seemed likely I inherited his behaviors.

She dipped her head, her hair falling forward. "Thank you for telling me."

My mouth twisted downward as I eyed her hands clenched in her lap.

"It's a deal breaker, isn't it?"

"I-I don't know." She sounded dazed. Her eyes filled with tears. "You said…you said that about children before, but I thought you just didn't know me…I—I need to think. Please, Jake. This is all so fast." Her voice was quiet, too low.

"You and I, or the album?"

"All of it. I told you, I've never dated. And you're…well, you're an amazing man, but you're also Jake Etsam of Jackaroo, and your goals are so different from mine. You have bodyguards and don't even blink at singing a song on stage you've never practiced."

Bloody hell. We were. As in, *complete* opposites.

Silence permeated the space. I hated the distance expanding between us. Hated I'd caused the tear that spilled over her lashes. Hated how much I wanted to comfort her, hold her, make it better—because I knew I couldn't. I couldn't because my dad's genes lived in me.

She blew out a breath, gazing out the window. "Reporters keep calling me at work and on my cell," she said as we came up on her block. She twisted her fingers together. "They've asked me what it's like to be a widow, what I think about the wars." She looked up, her eyes tormented. "I don't know if I can be a…a famous person and offer opinions on something as personal as Dez's choice to go in the service—or the fallout of him dying because of that choice."

I parked the SUV in front of her building and cupped her chin and tilted her head toward me. "Does it matter that I don't want that responsibility either? I never did. I like playing in a band, sure, but this was never supposed to be my life."

She disengaged from my hold, her face tense and her eyes dark. "You dumped a lot on me just now, Jake. I've wanted a baby since I was in first grade. In fact, my mother, even Sam, say that's my primary reason for living."

"Can't you just…"

"No!" She swiped at her lashes. "My lullaby that you like so much? That was my attempt to give up the dream, but I-I can't. Since meeting you…" She huffed, then sniffled. "You've over-whelmed me with your generosity and your bodyguards. But you don't want a baby." She bit her lip but the quaver in her voice gave away the depth of her pain. "To be honest, I want a house full of kids."

Closing my eyes, I nodded. She needed space and time to figure out if she could see a path forward for us—that I under-stood because I needed the same when I was overloaded by new emotional stimuli.

I might give in to her needs but didn't mean I enjoyed the process. "May I call you?"

She tugged on one of her curls, more riotous thanks to the moisture. It stretched long before bouncing back into a tight kink that reminded me too clearly that I wanted to wrap my fist in her hair, tip her face back and kiss the bloody resistance out of this woman.

For better or worse, I wanted Ryn: her voice but also *her*. The sexy hair, the knowing brown eyes, lush breasts and bum. If only I could get her to see what I did.

Ryn hesitated, her hand on the seatbelt buckle. She popped the button, and my grumpiness surged. I didn't want Ryn to leave the car—not without telling me when I'd see her again.

"I don't think that's smart." Regret spilled from each word. "For what it's worth, I really like you," she said, her voice remained quiet. She swallowed hard. "That's part of why I'm not sure I can do the album. I…I want things with you, Jake. Maybe—no, definitely too much. Because…because the no-kids thing might well be a deal breaker."

I expected her to jump out of my SUV, but instead, she leaned in and cupped my cheek, pressing her lips to mine.

I pulled her in closer, hands splayed through her hair, as I devoured her mouth. I memorized the way she tasted, breathed, whimpered, and responded. I wanted the kiss to last forever—as I had with each of the kisses we'd shared.

Ryn pulled out of my arms and hopped from the SUV. She ran into the building, never looking back to see Isaac head into the building behind her. I texted him, asking him to be discreet since Ryn didn't want him 'round. He shot me a thumbs-up as he hung back, letting Ryn step through the large, glass door.

As she disappeared inside, my mood blackened further.

———◆———

I hated every second of the next ten days to the point even Murphy—the cheeky arse—commented on how irritable I'd become.

"Shove it," I'd growled into the phone six days after I'd last seen Ryn, placing a check mark next to *Call Back Detective Davenport to ensure SPD is working on Ryn's case.* She mightn't want to see me, but that didn't mean I couldn't take care of her, keep her safe—find out if Sam had a license plate to match the one that tried to mow Ryn down.

The detective, who worked Mila's stalker case, was the only law enforcement person I knew in Seattle. He'd promised to review the matter, even though such work was below his paygrade. I put another check next to *Send Detective D an edible bouquet.* The man liked his fruit. Not like I planned to begrudge him his five-to-nine.

"Mila says you can't come over till you play nice."

Much as I loved Mila, I had no intention of spending more time with her and my lovesick brother. Blimey, even their bird liked snuggles and long walks on the beach.

I had a woman to win over. Because this sickness in my guts? Wasn't getting better. In fact, with each day that passed, my innards ached worse.

"I wouldn't be in this bloody position if you hadn't stuffed my chances with your stupid 'join-me-on-stage' bullshit." I would, too, because I blurted out my deep-seated fear in the worst possible way, but I didn't plan to tell Murphy that.

"You reckon she's upset over that?" Murphy grunted then huffed. "Fuck that! We leave for Sydney this Friday. I'll go up there and talk to her. Make it right before we go."

"You can't, you arse. I told her I'd give her space. And I will. Because she bloody asked for it."

But Murphy, being Murphy, never did bother to listen. He took Mila to the same Monday class I attended the week before—on the pretext of showing Mila the program.

When I saw the picture on social media later that day, rage and despair filled me, so I changed into my workout clothes and pumped iron until my muscles quivered and sweat ran in thick runnels down my chest and back—my new daily routine since Ryn cut me out of her life. I might not have stopped even then, but Alan threatened to punch if I didn't stop abusing my body.

Smart call, but I still hated Alan. And Murphy And my bloody sense of chivalry and decency that required me to wait for Ryn to let me back into her life.

Not that we hadn't spoken—we had because I couldn't *not* text her. But I hadn't heard her voice—a voice I craved—and I missed her.

Like last Thursday, I ordered ramen from a street vendor and texted her the picture. She responded that place was her favorite. I asked Ryn her student's favorite tonal pattern that class and she sent me a recording of the kids' singing "This Little Light of Mine." I found one of her mittens in my car, and she admitted she'd knitted that pair.

One night as we lay in our separate beds, she told me via text of her love for tulips and black-and-white movies. As of this morning, I knew she liked to go blackberry picking.

The more we shared, the more I wanted to share.

But Ryn didn't ask me over. In fact, she completed each text with *It's probably best for us to stop talking.*

Today, ten days after Ryn fled my vehicle, I scowled as Mila and Murphy headed into the airport, heads close together, looking forward to their three weeks with my mum back in Oz. I shoved the car into gear and headed toward Asher's studio, determined to work around my anger and my need—to finish the bloody album on schedule and budget.

Because I couldn't sit around and pine for Ryn any longer.

CHAPTER ELEVEN
Ryn

No doubt left in my mind—I missed Jake. Missed those intense hazel eyes and his strong shoulder made for my cheek. I missed his warmth and his clean, woodsy scent. But most of all, I missed Jake's comments, insights, thoughtful gestures. *I missed him.*

Was this what falling in love felt like? I'd never done this… whatever it was. My love for Dez grew out of our friendship and proximity and…expectations—both his parents' and mine.

But what I felt for Jake brewed bigger with each day I refused to let him back into my life. My hands jittered. My face flushed and my body tightened with need when I recalled our kisses. The past two nights, I'd lain awake as my body ached for him.

I settled out front of Linda's door as soon as my lunch break started, my hands wrapped tight around the to-go cup, the peppermint scent teasing me. No wonder Linda begged me to drink her coffee—I wasn't sure if I could withstand the delicious smell much longer.

"Hey, Ryn! Whatcha doing here this afternoon? I thought you'd be out with your rocker hottie."

I thrust the cup into her hands. "This is for you. And that's why I'm here. I-I messed that up. I haven't seen Jake in days."

Linda lifted the cup to her mouth and drew a long gulp. She smacked her lips and hummed. "Heaven. Explains the lack of new photos of you two. Come in. I have an hour before my next class. I'm assuming you wanted to talk about whatever's running through your mind?" She raised her brows as she took another greedy sip.

I followed her into her office and collapsed into the hard, wooden chair. "I don't know where to start, exactly." I blew out a breath. "Actually, I do. I don't think I was ever in love with Dez. I mean, I loved him and I miss him, but I wasn't *in love* with him—like you read about or see in movies or whatever. And… and I think he knew it because he felt the same way. That's why he didn't want to have a baby with me. Maybe he did that last tour because he didn't want to hurt me by telling me no again…" I swiveled my jaw, trying to get the thoughts and words to mesh. "I think that's why he joined the Army in the first place. Because he knew we weren't going to last."

Linda settled into her chair, crossing her ankles over the corner of her desk as she nursed the rest of her drink.

When she didn't say anything, I blurted out, "Sam might have been behind the attempted hit-and-run and destroying the guitar Dez gave me. I think…I think if I move on now, she'll have to accept Dez is dead, and she isn't ready."

Linda dropped her feet and leaned forward, setting the cup on the edge of her desk. "Let me ask you something. Who cares?"

I blinked, leaning back away from Linda's harsh voice and narrowed eyes.

She thumped her fist on her desk. "Who *cares* what Sam thinks or feels? Besides Sam, I mean. She's not *your* problem— especially if she's trying to scare you or hurt you, which she has."

I twisted my fingers together. "He doesn't want kids."

"You've known Jake all of two, three weeks or whatever, and you've already brought children into the conversation?"

"He told me. He looked at my face when I held one of the infants in my room and he knew." I dropped my gaze, my heart still heavy over the loss of the dream I'd begun to spin in my head with Jake. "I think I'm falling in love with him."

Linda rolled her eyes. "You didn't need my advice, hon. You just needed to admit it to yourself. The kids, the family part, that all comes after." She raised an eyebrow. "At least I assume sex and kids come after feelings, but what do I know?"

I smiled. Linda might be abrasive at times, but she was also almost always right. "You are wise. Thanks. I'll bring you another coffee next week."

"You will not! My metabolism is slowing down now that I'm middle-aged." Her eyes took on a sly glint. "If you want to help me out, you'll bring me a shirtless picture of your boyfriend."

I shook my head but couldn't stop the chortle as I headed toward the door. "I'll see what I can do. Thanks, Linda. Have a good weekend."

"You, too. Details on Monday!"

I went by his hotel. Jake never told me where he was staying, but in this case, his being famous finally helped. I still freaked out at the pictures of me eating lunch with Jake and Murphy or holding hands with Jake at the tree-lighting ceremony that continued to pop up online. Since the first picture hit the Internet, bloggers—specifically young women—wrote cruel statements about my looks, age, and widowed status. Yes, those comments played into my reasons for pushing Jake away. Which hurt me more than those mean-spirited bloggers.

More fool I.

His fame helped now, though. Or would have, if the desk agent, a tall brunette who stood behind the stacked-stone desk flanked by another large pine tree dripping with large red ornaments, helped me out. She didn't, even though I'm sure she knew who I was thanks to all the media attention these past two week. She smiled a tight, almost snarly grin and informed me, "Jake Etsam is not on my list."

Wow. Dating, even being married to Dez, women coveted him, sending me *how'd-you-land-him* looks, but until now, I'd never seen jealousy or whatever that was up close. Yet another daunting problem to tackle if Jake and I started dating.

Were we dating?

I broke down and texted him as the desk agent—Rebecca—spoke, and Jake responded as I walked across the fancy wood floor, my steps echoing back toward the enormous stone fireplace—its mantle festooned in fresh-cut pine boughs and red ribbons.

Wanted to talk to you.

I'm at the studio, finishing up with Pres. May I swing by after I finish up here?

I smiled at his eager response.

Please do. I've missed you.

"Thanks, Rebecca."

"Happy to assist," she replied, a small smirk on her face.

Isaac sauntered up to the desk behind me and tapped the counter. When she met his eyes, hers widened. "I bet," he said.

Then, before I had a chance to react, Isaac took my elbow and led me toward the exit.

"Ms. Hudson!" Rebecca called, her voice vibrating with urgency.

"I knew she knew who I was," I muttered at Isaac.

"Just keep walking. She's in trouble already and no point in helping her out now."

I glanced up at Isaac, whose lips pressed into a firm line. "In trouble why?"

"'Cause Jake's not gonna like how this played out."

I shivered but it wasn't so much from the cold as it was from a realization. "You've been with me this whole time, huh?"

"Yep."

"Is Jake safe with just Alan?"

Isaac opened my car door and raised his eyebrow. "Better to have both of us with him, but you're important. Jake knows that—and wants to protect you."

I handed Isaac the keys to my car. "You drive."

My head was too full of thoughts of Jake—of what I needed versus what I wanted—to focus on the road.

Isaac smiled as he ushered me around the passenger side and opened my door.

———

After Isaac dropped me off at my door, I took a long shower, used my best leave-in conditioner, smoothed and scrubbed my skin. Next, I heated up some soup I'd made earlier in the week during my Jake-free time and sat at the bar, straining to hear his footfalls in the hall. I'd eaten and cleaned up before he knocked a couple of hours later.

I flung the door open and stared at him.

"Hi." This time, even more than the first, Jake stole my breath.

This, my angel-man, I wanted more of these emotions with him.

He took in my long, beachy waves I'd spent over an hour messing with and my soft makeup as he leaned against the door frame. "You look good."

"Not as good as you. I almost forgot how much I like looking at you."

His lips curled upward—not quite a smile. More of his humor restored. "Can't have that, can we?"

I waved him in, but he didn't move from the door. Instead, he leaned forward and kissed me. This kiss was deep, and I brought my hands up to his wrists, holding him there as he plundered my mouth.

Jumping June bugs. I liked Jake kissing me. No, no. I *loved* kissing him.

He pulled back in slow increments, his eyes warm but wary. "That's how I like to greet you. Feel free to greet me the same way."

I brushed my fingertips over my swollen lips and nodded.

He straightened and stepped into my place, closing the door with a finality that caused my heart to flutter faster.

"Where's Alan?"

"With Isaac." Jake's gaze slashed to mine, nearly ruthless as it stripped me bare. "You going to tell me what you were thinking?"

Something in his demeanor seemed predatory—dangerous. I licked my lips, trying to figure out how to approach him.

Nothing came. I sucked in a breath and went with honesty. "You frighten me."

Jake's eyes softened but his arms remained crossed over his chest. "What are you scared of, love?"

I turned my back on his knowing eyes and moved into the

middle of my living room, but I remained too antsy to sit. Instead, I made a tour around my furniture.

"Not you. What you make me feel. For you." I paused, sifting my thoughts and emotions to explain the truths I'd stumbled onto this week. "Since meeting you, I've questioned my feelings for Dez. You heard his sister—Dez is kinda sacrosanct. Because he died, mainly, but also because everyone doted on him. Me included." The words rushed out faster and faster. "But much as I loved him…" Jakes eyes shuttered as his jaw clenched. "Maybe I wasn't the right woman for him. I've been working toward that conclusion for a while." I hesitated, but I'd gone this far. "That's what writing, singing 'A Moonlit Serenade' was. My emotional cleansing."

"That longing, then, is it for Dez?" Jake asked.

I shook my head, sucking on my bottom lip. Why was this so hard? "It's for the child I've always wanted."

"Tell me why."

"Why I want kids?" I shoved my hands through my hair, considering. No, I wasn't ready to go that far. "I just always have."

Jake's eyebrow shot up at my words, but he stayed silent.

Annoyance began to mingle with fear that he didn't want to put in the work of dealing with me and my baggage. Still, I needed to change the subject. Fast.

"I get that I can't control everything, but I need to have more say over my life than I did with a military husband, who set his deployments without input from me. I need to decide where I work and who I date and…" I trailed off at the sadness sliding over his features.

He rubbed his palm across his cheek, and I heard the light

scrape of his scruff against his skin. "Right. I can see why you'd worry about that. I'm not a control freak. Never have been. You're capable of taking care of yourself."

He narrowed his left eye into this sexy squint that made my thighs quiver. "Except with you," he murmured. "I like being in charge with you. Not because I want to own you." His words were slow as though he was reasoning this out as he spoke. "But because I care about you and want you safe and happy."

He rubbed the back of his neck, which caused his biceps to flex against his T-shirt. His gaze sought mine and the vulnerability there shocked me. *I want you safe and happy.* I believed him.

"I've never loved a woman before. Never fallen in love." He stepped nearer, his footfalls a metronome of change.

"I bet it's the same for you."

He waited for me to shake my head.

"But I think…I think that's what I'm doing here. And, Ryn, it scares me, too. I'm not ready for a bub." He raised his hand when I opened my mouth. "Yet. We don't know where we will go. So… so…maybe we muddle through together. And I can live with that for now—as long as we're together." His big hands wrapped around my waist, tugging me nearer to him. "Because I've hated every minute of these days apart, and I don't want to do that again."

"I missed you." My eyes filled with tears that I blinked back. Nothing really had changed. I wanted Jake but his life, his dreams differed from mine.

"Can you give me that? A few months to see if we fit? Then…" He swallowed, his jaw flexing as his hands tightened around my biceps. "Then maybe…well, let's just see how we do."

I bit my lips and Jake's face turned stormy. "Are you sure you want to do…whatever this is with me? I'm a mess. You can have any women you want—"

"Stop right there. I want *you* as my girlfriend. Only you."

I'd googled him this week—too much time and too much desire for him. Jake hadn't had a serious girlfriend since his junior year of college when he dated another art student for a few months. The previous women linked to him were "dates" or "friends," an interesting classification for a famous rocker. Warmth spread through me as I realized what Jake had said. I was his girlfriend—his first serious relationship in years.

I pulled his head down and kissed him, because I needed to, and because I would never get enough of the feel of his lips gliding over mine.

"I'll do the album."

At my words, Jake pulled back. Those piercing eyes lay half-hidden behind his drooping lids. His lips were wet from my kisses. His newly acquired scruff teasing and soft against my sensitized palm.

Jake huffed, dropping his forehead against mine. "You sure?"

"That scares me, too. Because I get that my life will change in ways I can barely imagine. But…but that has nothing to do with us. Together, I mean."

"Oh, it has everything to do with us together." He leaned closer with a growl and nipped at my jaw. My knees weakened and he tightened his arm around my waist.

"I'll do the album whether you want to be with me or not. I pushed you away, and I'm sorry, but I want to be with you. If you still want me."

"Think I proved I want you, too. Thrilled to have you on the album. Ecstatic. Now can I get back to kissing you?"

I slid my fingers through the top of his long, unruly hair. "Yes, please."

But he didn't kiss me. He stared at me with those eyes that ripped my soul to shreds and stitched me back up—all in one heartbeat. His confidence built with whatever he saw in my eyes. He stood taller, more in charge. My breathing grew shallower in response.

"I want to take you to bed, Lauryn. And I want to love you all night long."

Heat bloomed across my skin as I nodded.

"With words. I want to hear you say you want me, too."

"I want you," I breathed.

I stood on my tiptoes and brought my lips up to his, molding my body and my mouth to his harder planes. His fingers speared through my hair, tugging me tighter to him so our teeth clashed. I moaned, unable to hold back the onslaught of desire pulsing through my body, sending heat to pool in my lower abdomen.

His hardness pressed against my stomach and I reveled in his hunger. Jake's hand splayed across my lower back, right above my bottom, pulling me even tighter into his embrace. Our kisses turned ferocious in their need. Ten days was too long apart.

Somehow, my shirt was off, and Jake flicked the clasp on my bra, sliding the straps down my arms as he trailed soft kisses down my throat. This man, his raw masculinity tamed by this sweetness, caused my breath to catch and my body to warm further. I tugged at his shirt, desperate for the feel of his bare skin against mine.

He stepped back and pulled his shirt over his head in one

smooth, lithe movement. I gasped at the sight of him—tanned skin, firm, hard pecs trailing into a taut, ridged abdomen. I traced the sculpted muscles, my fingers tingling as they drifted over his hot flesh.

"You're beautiful," he said, his voice low and pulsing with the lust that clogged the air between us. His palm covered my breast and I arched my back, needing more pressure against the sensitive bud.

"Bugger it," he muttered, lowering his head to suck on my other nipple.

"What?"

"Wanted to talk it out, but you've got me so bloody famished for you, I can't think."

"Anything specific?"

His hands on my hips tightened, as if he feared I'd pull back. He raised his eyes and met my gaze, his serious.

"I told you about my father. That's my role model. That's what I know of fatherhood. Hiding in the back of a cupboard and putting my hands over my ears because my dad was drunk and mean. Can't continue that cycle, Ryn. It's bloody awful."

I covered his fisted hands with mine, bringing our joint arms up until I placed his hands on my chest.

"How old were you?"

"Just a mite. Three, I think."

I digested that while he opened my hands, palms warming from my body's heat. "Dez left me a month after our wedding. To go to basic training. I never had a choice in his decision because he signed up while I was at class."

His hands started to fist again, but I pressed my palms against the back of his, holding them to my body. "I've never said that aloud before. Never told anyone." I met his gaze; his filled with the same vulnerability I'm sure flashed through mine.

"I want to…blimey…I…can see me, holding you in bed, loving you every night for years. But kids? That's more than I…"

Sweat pooled at his temples and into his sideburns.

"Do you think Murphy will be a good dad?"

"Too right. He wants this nipper. Bad. Loves the baby like he loves Mila—single-minded in his focus. Never seen him so broken up as when he found out that bub Mila miscarried was his."

Someone once told me the fastest way to understanding was through the back door. "And you were raised in the same house? Had the same experiences?"

Jake's lips parted and his eyes shone with a different emotion. A better one. I leaned up and kissed him before he could say anything else. We'd talked enough for now.

"I'm going to say something to you I've never said before." I kept my voice light, though I was dead serious. "I want you to make love to me, Jake."

His lids lowered as his face transformed, sharpening, with lust. "You're all I think about. I fantasize about your skin, flushed with pleasure, your voice as you come."

With a boldness I never knew I had, I reached down and cupped him through soft denim, molding him to my hand.

Jake hissed a curse, his hips bucking.

"I meant it when I said I missed you," I said against his lips.

"I missed you, too. Murphy called me a whingeing arsewipe."

"Were you?"

"Reckon."

I'd never wanted like this—a raw, driving need that frightened me even as I yearned for more.

I couldn't get enough of his hair, the silky texture, as the strands locked around my fingers—another connection between us. He bent, biceps flexing, as he scooped me into his arms.

With long, sure strides, he carried me into my bedroom, laying me down on my bed. He settled next to me, head in his palm, as he stared at me with reverence. Using his index finger, he trailed a path from my lips, down my throat, to my chest, circling one nipple. I shivered, goose bumps raising, as my body responded to him.

I wanted to kiss him, so I did. Jake's lips parted as mine approached, and his days-old scruff tickled my lips and chin as our tongues touched, swirled, and delved. I moaned as his palm skimmed over my stomach and into the waistband of my leggings. His palm cupped my hipbone, his fingers pressed into the side of my bottom.

I shifted, swinging my leg over his hips and settling on top of him as he twisted to lay on his back.

His hands romanced my back as my palms cupped his cheeks, holding him where I wanted him while I sank deeper and deeper into the kiss—into Jake. Long minutes later, Jake pushed up, his abs flexing in the most delicious way, as he set me to the side. He stood, too, and with slow, easy motions, he removed the rest of my clothes.

Moonlight from the open window drifted over us as he touched and tantalized his way across my skin. I burned with a fever caused and only cured by Jake. Impatient, I reached down and undid his button, the rasp of his zipper exciting me, making me press against him as his fingers drifted up my inner thigh to my throbbing center.

"Please," I murmured.

"I'll love your sweet body, Ryn. When you're ready." His fingers eased inside me and my breath caught somewhere between a gasp and a sob. Slow, easy—Jake's way—he filled me with his finger before retreating. Again and again, he stroked me, readying my body for his.

I pushed my hands inside the waistband of his pants, and I trailed my fingertips up and down the thin streak of hair below his navel and above his boxer briefs. They were red. Sexy.

Jake added a second finger inside me, and I cupped his bulge again, gulping at its size. I massaged him through his underwear for a moment before building up the courage to slide my hands under his waistband and pushing his boxer briefs off his hips.

"I love the way the moonlight kisses your skin. Soft. Dreamy. Sexy as fuck."

His words made me whimper again. His fingers curled forward and hit that spot—the one that caused my knees to buckle and my brain to short circuit.

"Don't stop," I panted.

"Don't plan to. Not till you beg me to, anyway."

I wrapped my hand around the base of his thick erection, squeezing. Jake moaned, pressing himself more tightly into my hold. I pulled forward, letting my hand glide up toward his tip, my thumb flicking at the drop of moisture there.

"Hope you're ready, woman, because I can't bloody wait a moment longer."

"Yes. Now."

He eased me back onto the comforter and I lay there, nearly boneless with pleasure and anticipation.

"What do you want me to do?" I asked.

"Be you." He kissed one cheek. "Tell me what you like. What you want." He kissed my shoulder.

He stepped back from the bed and I shivered, trying desperately not to think of Dez, who had no place in this moment whatsoever. But that's what came from being with the same boy my whole life—I compared every experience with a man to Dez. Most had come up lacking. But Jake...I was beginning to believe Jake showed me just what a real man could—should—be.

He pulled out a condom and rolled it down his considerable length. My body clenched at the realization he was going to be in me.

"What are you worrying on?"

"Nothing."

Jake eased his knee onto the bed.

"Spill it, blondie. Or I won't do you."

I smiled, shaking my head. Jake was good at that—breaking tension and making me laugh.

"Just that you aren't Dez. You're you—and it's sexy and scary and...and hot as hell to have you here, in my bed."

He eased his body over me. "I gotta tell ya, love. I don't want you to make comparisons between us. When I'm here—it's just me. And you. Can you do that? For me?"

"That's what I'm trying to tell you." I rubbed my hand over his sun kissed brown scruff. "You're all I think about. All I want."

"Best words I ever heard." Jake kissed me, slow and sweet and so damn hot, I panted with need.

He glided over me, his muscles smooth and sensual as they slid across my belly and breasts.

"I'm going to love you now, Lauryn."

I slid my hands upward into his hair.

He worked his hand into my hair and made a fist, tugging my head back and exposing more of me to his mercy. He kissed my throat, sucked and nibbled at my breasts. "You're mine, Lauryn. Say it."

This alpha side of Jake shocked me. But in the best possible way. He waited, eyes burning into mine, his thick erection nudging my aching entrance. I shifted wanting more, but he pulled back.

"I'm yours, Jake."

"Right you are." And he brought his hips forward to plunge into me. I took him—all of him—and I keened at the heavy weight of his body sliding into me, over me.

"Yes, yes, yes," I chanted.

"Too right," he growled.

I pulled his head down for another kiss, and he obliged, taking my mouth with the same thoroughness as he took my body. His tongue speared into my mouth as he settled into a steady, intense rhythm.

I wanted to writhe against him, but his hips pinned me down, circling in small increments, grinding against my engorged clit.

"Oh!" I orgasmed. Hard. Harder than I could remember. And it went on and on as Jake circled his hips. He was relentless in his push to wring every drop of pleasure from my body.

I finally settled back, sated. He gazed down at me, a thin sheen of perspiration covering his skin, making him even sexier if that was possible. Inside me, his erection throbbed.

"You'll do that again before I come."

And he kissed me like I was the very air he needed to breathe.

My last—only—coherent thought was when he focused on a goal, Jake Etsam was a force.

One I wasn't sure I could withstand.

CHAPTER TWELVE
Jake

Ryn's eyes were dazed, slumberous as she stared up at me. When I nipped her ear, she moaned again, pressing her gorgeous breasts into my chest as she clenched tighter on my raging hard-on. I slid a hand behind her back and pulled her hips back to mine.

Her eyes widened with shocked pleasure as the next burst of sweet, hot desire flooded her body. I planned to keep her in this state as often as possible. I loved her like this.

"I want you to scream my name."

She murmured a response as my lips crashed down on hers.

I wasn't sure where my assertiveness came from, all I knew was that Ryn brought it out of me.

I caressed her, learning what she liked—how hard to nip and pinch—where to kiss and nibble. The hotter she burned, the hotter I did, too.

Ryn did scream my name. Twice. Second time, I couldn't hold back any longer, and I bellowed her name as my body exploded with wave after wave of pleasure. My release complete, I took a minute, to rest my head on Ryn's shoulder before I found the energy to roll over, taking her with me. Our connection remained.

I ran my hand down her back, keeping the touch light. She shivered, snuggling closer.

"Cold, love?"

"A little. Only my back. You keep the rest of me toasty."

I maneuvered my hand down and managed to disentangle our limbs from the bedclothes. With a firm tug, I covered us both.

"Do my best."

We lay there, hearts calming and bodies easing into each other.

She lifted her head and I ran my fingers through those long, thick curls, loving how the moonlight caught in the gossamer-thin palest strands. *As if spun by moonlight. Soft but warm. There she is, smiling down, filled with the joy that our love was born.*

The lyrics that flooded my mind caught me off guard, but I considered the imperfect rhyme. Never been one for songwriting before—that was Murphy and Hayden's role.

Still…I liked it. Ryn's hair fascinated me—the myriad tones, the thickness, the softness.

"It's a mess," she said on a sigh, frowning at her hair's tangles.

"I like it this way. My favorite, actually."

She glanced away, but not before I saw the worry building in her eyes. "Was that…did you enjoy that?"

Hadn't she heard and felt my response to her?

"Will you look at me?" I waited until she did, though my heart began to thunder against my ribs and a cold sweat popped out on my skin.

She sucked in a breath and raised her gaze to mine. Hers remained darker, full of shadows where I only ever wanted to see light.

"That was the single best experience of my life. Bar none."

She shook her head. "It's okay, Jake. I know I'm not…You've been with other women, and I…Dez was it for me. I mean, I liked sex, but it just never…I've never experienced anything like what we did before." She finished in a rush, her cheeks flaming pinker than a cockatoo's feather's.

"Good." At her startled look, I continued, "I haven't either.

131

What we did here, in your bed, was us, being us." I maneuvered, finally pulling out of her soft, tight clench. I gritted my teeth, wanting nothing more than to bury myself back inside her.

I would, but first Ryn needed reassurances. Those I could give her.

"I've never pillow-talked so dirty before," I said. "Ever. But with you, I couldn't help it."

Her lips parted as she stared at me, eyes wide. Did a man's ego good, that look. I planned to keep it on her face.

"Did you like what we did together?" I asked.

She nodded.

"Did you like the way I touched you? The way I filled your body?"

Her cheeks flamed again, and this time the blush spread down her neck to her breasts. Blimey, I needed to feel her skin while she blushed like that. I lowered my lips to her throat, moaning at the contact.

"I did. I do like the way you touch me. I like you being in charge while we're in here." Again, she was hesitant. I waited, but I couldn't resist bringing my hand up to cover her flushed breast. Her skin was smooth but soft, warm. Filled with vibrancy and the smell of Ryn—and me. My body zinged with need.

"It's just…" She played with my hair. She did seem to have a fascination with it. Whatever got her going.

I nuzzled into the valley between her gorgeous globes. I loved her breasts.

"You make me feel beautiful and…and hot. I burn with you."

I rolled her over onto her back, unable to resist her a moment longer. I crawled up her body, kissing and licking my way to her mouth, which I took and plundered.

"Best answer. I'm going to make you burn again. Now."

"Will you...will you stay?"

Her eyes pleaded but her voice was steady. I had no clue what she was thinking, but once again, I knew I must reassure her. I cupped her cheek, my thumb drifted over her plump, damp lip. "There's nowhere I'd rather be."

Her smile lit up her face, her eyes glowing, all those shadows burned away with my words.

A small niggle of unease crept up my spine, but I ignored it, opting to kiss her lush mouth once again.

This, here, was heaven. *Our* moonlit serenade. Heaps different from her song, but I planned to play—and enjoy— every bloody note.

———◆———

"Where were you today?" Ryn asked as she snuggled against my shoulder. I lay on my back, sprawled across the bed as I'd been since my trip to the loo after our second round of love-making.

She liked touching. I frowned. From what I'd seen, she didn't get much contact outside the nippers she worked with. Must be lonely, then.

"I went by your hotel."

My arm wrapped tight around her narrow waist. She might be slight but Ryn was stacked with luscious breasts—worthy of any master sculptor. I wanted to spend hours worshipping her bum with my hands and mouth. Soon, I decided.

I shifted because part of my anatomy refused to offer Ryn's

body a rest. Plus, she wanted to talk, and I was happy to oblige. I wanted to tell her about my day, hear her thoughts and concerns about her own.

"Isaac told me. You're on my approved list, by the way. Added you right after I met you."

"Well, the tall dark-haired lady at the front desk didn't seem to think so."

I smiled at Ryn's frustration—more like jealousy. Never wanted to be the object of a jealous lover before. Now I did.

"I've already put a call in to the manager about the front desk clerk's stunt today. I was at Asher's studio. Preslee finished her songs this afternoon. Asher and I started mixing one. We think Pres will sing the opener, then Ash, then maybe our duet. Can't tell till we hear some of how you and I work together, but after I laid my track and first round vocals, we went over the production schedule. We're three songs short of a full EP."

Ryn digested what I told her, considering her place in my world, no doubt. Now that I understood her better, I could wait for her to come to the decision on her own—she'd been learning these past two years how to be independent and she deserved my vote of confidence in her abilities.

"Has Isaac been following me this whole time?"

"Yes."

"Why?"

"Because someone tried to kill you."

She stiffened beside me—every muscle rigid. "That's not how I remember the situation." Her voice serrated at the end of the words, cutting into my languor.

"Ryn, I have the means to protect you. I brought you into

my world—that's why Isaac's tailing you and that's why I spoke to a detective."

"What?"

Uh-oh. This time I couldn't mistake the anger in her voice. Her eyes, when she lifted her head, were wide with anger.

"I just mentioned it to the detective who worked on Mila's case. We're mates." An overstatement, but Ryn's demeanor told me I was well on my way to getting kicked out of her bed.

She blew out a breath in slow increments. "Sam's dad will talk to her."

"And if he doesn't? What if he doesn't believe you? What then? This is your safety." She opened her mouth to argue, but I placed my index finger over her lips. "Please, *please* think about what you'd want if our positions were reversed."

She snapped her lips together, her eyes still shooting angry darts at mine. And, just like that, I stuffed up—why'd I have to mention that now?

Because I'd been thinking about her self-sufficiency, and I wanted her to know I'd take care of her. But…more fool I… Ryn didn't want to be taken care of. She wanted to prove herself. Needed to prove herself.

"I'm sorry you're upset. I wanted to help you, not make you angry."

Again, she nodded. She lay down, but the ease between us vanished. Because of my big, fat mouth.

———

"What are your plans today?" I asked her over breakfast the

next morning. She made something called a breakfast burrito.

This Yank food proved delicious. Sausage, eggs, potatoes and some gooey cheddar wrapped in a whole-wheat tortilla. Yep, made my taste buds dance.

"I have a class at eleven, one thirty, and three thirty, then I'd planned to drop off a donation at the synagogue tonight." She watched me with those careful eyes.

"May I come?"

Her smile grew as she nodded. "I assumed you'd have to do rock star stuff."

"I do."

Her shoulders slumped a bit.

I set my burrito down on the plate and bounced my leg, trying to figure out what she wanted from me. At least she wasn't angry anymore. A step in the right direction. Still, I needed to tread with care.

"I've got to be at the studio at nine, but after lunch, I'm going to rock out with nippers and my girl."

Ryn laughed. "Good save."

"Thought so."

"Does it bother you? Me celebrating both holidays?"

I leaned across the table and kissed those soft, sweet lips. My addiction to Ryn's mouth grew every day. Same with the rest of her, really, but it was her lips I fantasized about. Touching them, licking them, biting them, having her wrap them around my…I shifted, my pants as uncomfortable as the guilt now blanketing my shoulders.

"Of course not. Must have been fun growing up. Bet some of the kids were heaps jealous."

136

Ryn shrugged, still looking a bit twitchy. "Some. Others called me names, made fun of my Jewish heritage. That's part of why I keep celebrating." She paused, sucked in a big breath. "Why I want my children to learn and participate in Jewish culture and traditions." She peeked up at me from the side of her eyes.

"Right-o. Seems smart. And I like your attachment to your family, your history." I kissed her again, taking my time, dancing my tongue over her lips, wrapping it around hers before caressing the warm cavity of her mouth. "You'll have to teach me. I've never been to a Hanukkah celebration, and I don't want to muck it up."

She blinked her eyes open, those lips swollen and wet from my kisses. I pressed against her belly, bringing my hand to her back so she could feel my response to her.

"I'm not…" She shook her head, appearing to clear out some thought, leaving me to wonder what she'd been about to say. Her eyes pleaded with me to drop the topic. An uncomfortable feeling churned through my belly—as if Ryn was writing off a future with me because of the kids she wanted.

"If you want to go tonight, I'm in," I blurted, needing to move past this awkward moment.

"It's a menorah-lighting ceremony at the local community center. I normally drop off a couple of care packages for the homeless. Sing a few songs."

I crossed my arms over my chest. "You don't leave a bloke much time to organize, do you?"

Her lashes fluttered down to cover her eyes. "I wasn't sure you'd want to go. And it's not like we were really talking until last night."

"If this is important to you, then I want to participate."

She remained stiff, unsure how to respond, but her eyes, when she met my gaze, were full of longing.

Yet another wall to scale—to conquer—to prove my interest in her. "Did Dez do these things with you?" I asked, the certainty of her answer already building like a wildfire in my gut.

"Sometimes. I mean, he liked the 'Dreidel Song.'" She smiled but it was forced. "But he wanted me to focus on his family's traditions. Those were familiar."

When she pulled back, I ran my hands down her spine, cupping her hips. "Your past makes me jealous. I reckon I'll learn to handle that."

Ryn blinked up at me, her honey-colored brows tucked in tight over her nose. "You've dated women—beautiful women— for the past few years. I can't compete with them."

I pinched her chin between my thumb and forefinger. "You don't have to. I didn't date much—too bloody shy around all that skin, first off. Left me tongue-tied and stupid."

Ryn's frown deepened, but I pressed on.

"They wanted Murph anyways. I'm the quiet one. Not much interest in me when they could have the bad boy. But my point was that I wasn't involved with many of them—didn't want to end up like my brother, the wanker."

"You're telling me you were too sweet and shy for sex?" Skepticism dripped from Ryn's voice. I'd painted myself into this corner, and had no clear way out.

"Well, not exactly." Blimey, my cheeks and ears burned. "I mean, I did have sex with some of those women."

Ryn stiffened and pulled back as I rushed on, my heart hammering as I stumbled over the words I needed to say. "But we both knew it wasn't a long-term deal. I mean, I was only in town for a day, sometimes two." I stopped talking, my hand running through my hair as my guts twisted and yanked into greater discomfort. "I'm really mucking this up."

Ryn wrapped her arms around her middle. "This right here is part of what I struggle with. Why I tried to get you to leave when we first met. I don't like the idea of casual sex. I've never practiced it, and while you're harping on my marriage, I'm thinking about all the women you've been with who didn't mean anything more than a quick release."

I sighed. "That's my point. There haven't been that many. I'm not like Murphy."

I stepped closer, but Ryn held herself and her ground, making me work for the closeness I craved with her—*only* her. How to explain that? How to get her to see it?

"I'm not a bloody monk, but I haven't had a girlfriend in years. Haven't wanted one because to me, it's about caring. I care about you, Ryn. More now that we've been together." I touched one of her curls, tugging it gently before tucking it behind her ear and caressing her cheek.

Ryn's lashes fluttered down but not before hurt filled her pretty eyes. While I understood her desire for more, I'd never been one to lie. I wouldn't—not with Ryn.

Though, in that moment, I wondered if I'd just cost myself the one woman I'd be able to love.

CHAPTER THIRTEEN
Ryn

Jake met me after lunch for my early afternoon class—which was filled with the same number of freak-outs as the Monday moms, but once we did all the requisite selfies and autographs, class went smoothly. We had one more week of musical fun time before the winter break, which lasted a full month.

Every spot in my spring classes was filled, and I received several requests for new children each day, probably thanks to Jake's presence and also Murphy Etsam showing up with his fiancée last week as to do with my teaching skills.

Both times I saw them together, I envied Mila's ease with Murphy. Their dynamic fascinated me: his impulsivity tempered by her thoughtful review. Mila might be quiet, but she was assertive—something I appreciated more now that I'd fully considered Dez's actions and my acquiescence to his plans.

Jake and I managed to snag one of the studios after class, in the hour before my next one.

"You want to do 'A Moonlit Serenade' last?" he asked.

I nodded, fiddling with my guitar strap. "Is that okay? I mean, I just want some more direction before Asher dissects my song." The song I wrote to the child I'd never have with Dez. If I stayed with Jake, I might never have a child, period. I fiddled with the knobs, retuning the strings—anything to busy my hands and help me ease the ache in my chest.

"How about we start with 'All the Pretty Little Horses'? See how that sounds with your guitar?"

I nodded and began to strum out the melody. Jake gestured

for me to begin. I closed my eyes, still unused to having a musician of Jake's caliber watch me as I sang. I startled, missing a note, when he matched my pitch for the chorus. I opened my eyes and looked deep into his as I sang the next verse. He sang the chorus again and I finished the last verse.

He smiled, his eyes alight with pleasure. "Blimey. You're a dream to work with. If we're that on point for our first rehearsal, this is going to be the fastest album I've ever worked on."

"Really?" I asked.

"Fair dinkum. You've no idea how unprepared musicians can be coming into their studio time."

"Isn't that a waste of money?"

Jake shrugged. "Guess it doesn't matter so much when the studio's footing the bill."

I strummed out the opening chords again. "But you're paying for this one, right?"

"Yep."

"So, you're on the hook for the time and the marketing and whatever else goes into it?" I asked, my stomach once again cramping with nerves.

"Most of it, but Asher's been right decent about the studio time. We exchanged a larger percentage of sales on the record."

My palms turned sweaty. "I thought this is more of a personal project."

"It is." Jake tugged me closer to him, clearly sensing my unease. "But that doesn't mean it won't sell heaps of copies. Don't worry. You'll get your percentage. It's in the contract I brought over for you to sign."

"Okay." I didn't know what else to say.

"Can we run through the song again?"

I smiled, but it felt a little off. Talking sales and studio time was so outside my wheelhouse. I struggled to focus, wondering how Jake and I could possibly make us work.

Later that day, when my last class ended, I put my version of Mila's quiet will to work, insisting on walking home alone. I needed more time to process everything Jake brought to my life—the photographers who met me outside my apartment building each day, the questions and interest in me in the media, my changing role as a musician—it all slammed around in my head, but the most important question was how to reconcile my attraction to Jake with my desire for a family.

"Let me drop you off at least?"

I shook my head. "The exercise will do me good. I'll see you later tonight."

"Ryn. What's wrong?"

Trusting in life—as I had that Dez would return home, as he had the previous two times—proved stupid. If I didn't take the time now, didn't make my goals happen soon, they may not ever come true. I might not be a mom.

"Nothing," I said on a sigh.

Jake was more attuned to my needs than I gave him credit for, and his eyes filled with concern. "I care about you. I want you happy."

On some instinct I couldn't control, I leaned up and into him, kissed him, let him wrap those strong arms around me. We rested together, my ear pressed to his heart. But then I pulled back—from the embrace and from the emotions flooding through my system.

142

Maybe it was the magic of the season. Or, more simply, the yearning in my heart. I craved Jake's love. His touch made me near incoherent with desire. But his thoughts, laying bare his insecurities as I had many of mine, albeit unintentionally thanks to Sam and her crazy antics, left me feeling raw and unsure.

Once home and cleaned up from work, I parted my hair far to the right and braided the front section back, letting the ends pull through so it was an unstructured style—more to keep the wisps from my face—and pinned the ends with a few bobby pins. Overall, the look was casual but festive, especially after I tucked a few tiny, pink rosebuds from my one living plant into the style. I wore my favorite blue cashmere dress that hugged my curves and fell to mid-calf. I pulled on black tights and tucked my feet into my heeled black boots with the sassy silver decorations.

After many long moments of consideration, I wore my grandmother's pearl earrings but no necklace. The one that matched the dress and earrings had been a gift from Dez on our first anniversary, and wearing it—any mention of Dez—annoyed Jake. That level of jealousy still felt unwarranted, but I understood his dislike of my past being flaunted in his face.

My biggest fear, well, after the idea of dying alone, without anyone to miss me: I wasn't cut out to be a rock star's girlfriend. I wanted a loving marriage, a quaint home filled with music, laughter, and lots of kids, and a man I could always, always count on to come home to me at night.

Jake wasn't a good bet for any of those.

I sat on the edge of my bed and took deep breaths. Clearly, we were all wrong for each other.

My doorbell rang and I stood, forcing my back up to straight and my chin to a jaunty angle. We'd have tonight.

Then…then, I'd do what I needed to do.

Laughter and joyous voices spilled from the synagogue as we made our way up the steps. Jake took my hand, sliding his finger between mine. I swallowed down the ache in my heart at his simple touch, the easy affection.

Once we entered the building, we gave our coats to an elderly man. The man had no idea who Jake was, causing us both the relax.

We added our hygiene packs I'd purchased earlier to the donation table— Jake grumbling about how it was supposed to be his shout.

I ignored him and focused on the ebb and flow of the crowd.

"Ever tried a latke?" I asked.

Jake shook his head, so I led him over to the station of potato pancakes.

"Mazel tov!" The middle-aged lady said with a broad smile.

I eschewed the apple sauce but Jake added a bit to his plate, eyeing the pancake with skepticism. Biting into my latke, I enjoyed the crisp outer crunch and the soft, smooth potato center. Jake nibbled at his, his eyes brightening as he chewed. He dipped his latke into the apple sauce and grunted in appreciation.

Once we'd finished, he took our plates and threw them in the large black bins lining the back wall.

"Can you make latkes?" he asked.

"My grandmother taught me when I was very young."

Because my mother was too busy working to pay me any attention. "They're one of my favorites."

He clasped our hands together. "Mine, too. Can't wait for you to make me yours."

I dragged my gaze from his, unwilling to agree or get sucked in further to a conversation about my family. Lack of family, really. "Oh, look! There are the dreidels. Have you ever played?" I tugged him over, not waiting for his answer.

Thirty minutes later, Jake sang as he spun his blue plastic dreidel, eyes alight with pleasure when he won another piece of chocolate. He stood, offering this piece to me. I took it from his hand, my fingers brushing his palm.

The heat from our connection sizzled up my arm, making me shiver and my heart ache.

"Want to stay for the singing?" I asked, taking a bite of the chocolate. "Mm. This is good."

Jake rubbed the corner of my mouth, his eyes flaring with heat as he raised his thumb to his lips to suck off the crumb of chocolate that he had brushed off me.

My breath caught as he continued to look at me with those mesmerizing eyes. Finally, he lowered his hand to my hip and leaned toward my ear. "I learned the dreidel song and ate a latke. Can that be enough for tonight?"

My heart fluttered and I shivered. "Is there a reason you want to leave?"

He nuzzled his nose into my neck, pressed his lips to the delicate skin just under my ear. "Ryn, Ryn, Ryn. I want to take you back to your place, strip you out of that arse-hugging dress and shag you till morning." He pulled back just enough to meet my wide eyes. He leaned in until his lips almost touched mine. "M-maybe longer if you can s-s-s-stay awake."

My vocal cords froze, and I could only stare at him as he pulled me closer to his hard body. His eyes turned uncertain, much as his stutter proved his nervousness.

A child bumped into our legs, laughing. What was I doing? What was he doing to me? He just wanted sex, which he could get from almost any woman. But he asked me—wanted to be exclusive with *me*.

My heart pounded as I considered the fallout. Jake would hurt me. In the end, he'd leave. Everyone left me.

I had to make the choice now and live with the repercussions.

The "Dreidel Song" rolled around us. People's happy voices rose above some applause.

I wanted Jake. I wanted his body over mine—in mine. Taking him back to my place meant admitting my growing need for him.

I whispered one word that ensured my eventual broken heart. "Yes."

CHAPTER FOURTEEN
Jake

Ryn remained preoccupied throughout the day, but especially after we spoke more about the album. She pulled back, and I couldn't stand the emotional or physical space she wanted to build between us. Not now that I'd seen her in that dress. Not now that I knew how soft and supple her curves were underneath her clothes. I adored her flat tummy and small, puckered belly button. The flare of her hips, the slender line of her thighs. I craved her more with each passing second.

"Did you have fun?" I asked as we walked toward my SUV.

"Yes." Her breath slid from her mouth in small white puffs, almost like the fairy floss I loved to eat at a carnival. Nothing but spun sugar, that stuff—it was delicious. Not unlike Ryn's skin. "Though, to be honest, I don't really like the holidays."

I stopped her there, on the sidewalk, the moonlight pouring down over us with its silvery fae light. "Why ever not?"

"I guess because I never built my own traditions. Dez and I were only married for two of them. The rest I either spent alone or with friends."

"Why not spend it with his family?" I asked.

"I did when we were young, but his family's really into Christmas. I mean, Ted still dresses up like Santa on Christmas Eve. They had their own traditions, and as close as we were, I was always the outsider." She shook her head. "Plus it gets dark early, and it's cold. Better to just stay home."

"Tell you what. I'll take you to Sydney—no, the Gold Coast—next year. We'll surf all morning and eat a seafood feast right there on the beach." I wrapped my arm around her waist and began to stroll again. "You can lick wine from my abs. Always wanted to try that one." I winked.

She giggled, as I hoped she would. "You're a bad influence."

"I'm fun." I grinned at my next joke. "The fun-loving Etsam brother."

She shook her head, laughing harder.

I opened the car door for her and settled her in the seat. After settling in myself and starting the car, I said, "So what do you reckon? We got ourselves a date?"

She stiffened, her body preternaturally still—as if she scented danger. "You don't know where you'll be next December. I'll be here, teaching my classes, but you might be touring or recording or doing some PR thing or…whatever."

Oh, bloody hell. Ryn needed the assurance of long-term commitment. Much like I needed my mum so often after she booted my father. Dez abandoned Ryn, maybe not intentionally, but still. He left to fight in Iraq three years out of the five they were married. No wonder she expected the same from me. That's why she'd pulled back. That's why she wanted to protect herself.

I slowed for a red light, then turned to face her, my heart leaping and my tongue tied. She stared straight out the window but her pulse jumped in her throat. Seeing the physical manifestations of her confusion eased my own.

I ran my fingertips down her cheek and neck, loving the soft, warm velvet of her skin. The connection calmed me further— enough to speak. "Know what my mum used to say?"

Ryn turned her head and met my gaze.

"You make time for what's important. That's how you line up

your priorities. Since meeting you, you're tops on my priorities list."

Her smile bloomed brighter and she clasped my hand in hers. "Thank you for that. I worried."

A car honked behind me. Right-o. My turn. I held the wheel low with my free hand and punched the gas, enjoying this moment.

"What's the worry?" I asked.

She sat still and quiet for so long I doubted an answer. Finally, she spoke. "My parents weren't around much," she said, her voice hesitant and filled with pain. "They weren't concerned about what I had going on. I preferred to stay at Dez and Sam's."

"My mum worked a lot after she booted my father out. Difficult and scary at times, growing up alone. Well, I had Murph, but I understand your worry."

She nodded, her face still turned toward the window. I caught a glimpse of her reflection in the glass, and her mouth puckered with intense emotion. Something about her relationship with her parents still rubbed Ryn the wrong way. My breath caught in my lungs. Had her parents abused her? Was that why she spent so much time with her neighbors?

As soon as I put the car in park, she leaned over and kissed me, scrambling my thoughts and making me forget the questions I had for her when she ran her fingers up into my hair, pressing her soft breasts to my chest. I fisted my hand in her hair, and the kiss exploded.

Within seconds, I'd pulled her across the gearshift and yanked her dress high enough for her to straddle my hips. My hands roamed from her ribs down over her hips to clasp her high, taut bum. I rocked her back and forth against the zipper of my trousers, but I wanted more.

"We've got to stop." My voice came out guttural, more of a grunt. Probably because all my blood left my head and pooled in the heated, aching flesh pressing against my flannel dress trous. When she wiggled, my hips bucked upward, pressing against her, seeking her heat.

"Much as I love the kisses down my neck, we're in my car in the parking garage. I want you naked more than my next breath, but I don't want to embarrass you."

She raised her head, lips swollen, eyes heated with desire. I leaned forward and kissed her, keeping the touch light, soft, like a whisper. This time, I tucked her head against my chest, and held her until her heart rate slowed and my erection eased enough to find some comfort in my pants.

I sifted my hand through her long waves, loving how soft and warm her hair felt against my callused skin.

"Would you like to come up to my place?"

"Yes."

She giggled. "Quick with that one."

I rolled my eyes. "Didn't need to think about it."

Her breath puffed against my cheek before she scrambled out the driver's door. "Come on, then, stud."

I eased out of the car, then took her hand as we headed toward the bank of elevators.

"Got plans tomorrow?" I asked.

She shook her head.

"Wanna hang out?"

"When do you need me to start recording?" she asked.

"Next week. We're finishing laying down the instrumental and all my songs as well as Ash's. Pres added electric viola to hers and one of mine. Sounds good. I didn't know your full work schedule, but Asher said we should be able to work around it."

We stepped into the elevator.

"I'm off for a month after next week."

"That'll work perfectly." I grinned. "I'll let Ash know on Monday so we can start working on our songs in a week."

She pressed her hand to her stomach, eyes widening. "Oh my. I'm really going to meet Asher Smith."

"Too right, love."

"I may pass out."

"Wouldn't be the first time that happened."

"Or sing really badly because I'm nervous."

"That wouldn't be a first either."

She fidgeted. "I don't know how I let you talk me into this." She opened the door to her apartment and I followed, shutting and locking the bolt behind me.

"Yes, you do. You said my kissing drove you over the edge."

She removed her coat and threw it over the back of the couch. The dress clung tenaciously to her breasts. I wanted my hands on those soft-tipped globes. I wanted to suck those pretty pink nipples into my mouth, swirl my tongue, and bite just hard enough for her to mewl in pleasure.

"Will you take me to bed, Jake?" she asked, voice hesitating just enough for me to know she didn't ask that question often—if ever.

I smiled, liking her hesitation. Somehow, that added to my power—my role as in-charge. Yeah, this was good. *We* were good together. "I'd like nothing more."

"Will you…" She raised those big brown eyes to mine, hers vulnerable but also heated with desire. "Will you love me, Jake?"

I snaked my arm around her waist. "With pleasure." I bent down, my lips hovering next to her ear. "I promised you a night of passion, and I plan to deliver. Then I'm going to cuddle you close till you slip into slumber."

She wrapped her arms around my neck and slid up onto her tiptoes. "That all sounds great. But…"

I ran my hands over her arse, pulling her tighter to my hips, groaning at how good she felt. "What?"

She stepped back and unzipped her zipper. Pale creamy flesh glowed in the soft moonlight, highlighted by the slash of rose-pink satin bra and panty set.

"I can't wait for the bed."

I hauled her into my arms, my need matching hers.

I wanted it to be like this, just the two of us, forever.

I hoped it wasn't too much to ask.

CHAPTER FIFTEEN
Ryn

Since I'd made the decision not to boot Jake from my life the night at the synagogue, I waited for the perfection to wear off. Not that Jake was perfect—he tended to overthink everything, sticking to more cautious food choices or driving routes. Fine. I found those idiosyncrasies adorable. He liked to eat banana muffins with a strong cup of Earl Grey in the morning. He took up most of my queen-size bed…but he cuddled in close, keeping me both warm and safe in his arms.

Somehow, in a blink, my life took a sharp turn into fairy tale land a few weeks ago, and I loved—and feared—every minute of this new reality.

I called my doctor and reinstated my birth control prescription. Picking it up from the pharmacy the next day took more fortitude than I expected, but Jake asked me to give him time, and I'd promised I would.

Still, my heart ached a little each time I popped the pill. Yet Jake made up for that ache in so many ways.

Eating meals with him seemed normal as did our time in my apartment—he'd stayed over more nights than not. By that weekend, I couldn't stand it anymore.

"Why do you keep the suite at the hotel?"

"Because my clothes are there, and I need to practice my bass."

"But…you can do that here."

Jake paused, lifted his face toward my heated one. "You sure you're okay with me being here?"

"Um. Yeah. I mean, you are anyway. And the amount of

money you've shelled out for that hotel room you barely see makes me ill."

"I play my bass for hours, typically. And now I need to work on my voice exercises—when I'm not at the studio."

"My neighbors work most days and won't be here to hear you. And I'll need to be working with you on these songs."

Jake wrapped me in his arms. "I thought about buying a condo near you but I worried that would be presumptuous. Or that the places I looked at would offend your sensibilities, sending me back into that 'you people' category."

I shrugged. "I don't like to waste money. My parents worked hard to raise me in a nice neighborhood with good schools." But never gave me the one thing I needed from them: affection. So, yeah, I saw money as a tool—one I liked to stockpile. But I craved this closeness with Jake, which had more to do with my decision-making than I was willing to tell him. Yet.

Jake didn't love me. He might not ever even though we were more comfortable together than most couples I knew. Still, love didn't just spontaneously occur—at least not in my life. It built over time, with each new layer of trust and acceptance, laughter and cuddles.

But then, Dez said he loved me, and left.

I closed my eyes and rested my cheek against Jake's shoulder, my mind spinning on the same topic I had yet to fully grasp. Except that our relationship moved at light speed, and I couldn't figure out how to slow it down. Didn't want to, really. But…with speed came exceptional crashes. Big, fiery ones that destroyed everyone they touched.

"I get that. My mum did her best, but money was tight—too

154

tight—for years. Probably why I like tossing some of it now. But you're right. Squandering cash isn't my thing. I'll cancel the suite. And if it gets to be too much, I can bunk with Isaac and Alan down the hall."

I didn't say anything, but my shoulder tightness eased.

"I can't believe you were able to get a sublease here so quickly, and on this floor."

"Yeah. Funny how things work out sometimes." Jake hugged me closer to him, pressing a kiss to my temple. "And if you're a'right with me being here for a bit, I'll stay whilst I look for another place."

I sat back to pull my hair up into a loose bun, mainly to cover the building tremors in my hands. This conversation constricted my chest. "You really want a place in Seattle?"

"Fair dinkum." Jake threaded his fingers through my hair, loosening the bun until my waves tumbled down my back again. "Three of Jackaroo's members are here. My brother and his soon-to-be-wife plan to live here. I'm working on this album. Yeah. Makes sense to own a place. I'll be back and forth because of Murph and Mil if nothing else."

I swallowed and dropped my gaze. Jake homed in on my discomfiture and tilted my chin back toward him.

"Not that I think there's nothing else." He pulled me back into his arms and rocked me back and forth. "So, my Chrissie prezzie is to live with you. Damn good prezzie." He nuzzled into my neck, nipping at the sensitive spot where the soft skin met my shoulder. "Must have been heaps nice this year."

Jake, staying here, with me. Wow. Did that mean he cared more? Or was I convenient? I wanted him here, so did his reasons matter? I smiled, tried to pull off a flippant tone.

"I don't think what we've been doing together could be considered nice."

His smile formed in increments—and devastated my senses. As usual. This man managed to get me so hot and bothered, I forgot logic, let alone all the reasons he'd eventually leave. Or I'd leave him.

We hadn't talked about it since our reconciliation, but I still craved a child of my own. In fact, as the days inched closer to my twenty-seventh birthday, a mild panic set in.

"Since you're giving me everything I want, what can I give you?"

Jake's words tugged me from my inner turmoil. His face was beautiful, his piercing eyes steady on mine.

"You did. Detective Davenport spoke with Ted and Sam. All's good, thanks to you."

Jake shook his head, eyes never leaving mine. "You sorted that. Now, tell me. If you could have anything. And I mean *anything*. What would you ask for?"

"Fiji," I blurted. I dropped my gaze as my cheeks heated with my secret—one I'd never intended to admit. "I love the water. Those grass huts. The frangipani. Seems like paradise."

I stole a peek at Jake's face in time to see him press his lips together and nodded once.

"I assume you mean to visit. Be a bit pricey to purchase the island." He smiled. "But I did get you something else. Bit less flash."

He handed me a bag. Inside was a beautiful menorah. I'd told him last week I'd never owned my own since Dez didn't care to celebrate Hanukkah. I ran my fingertips over the hand-crafted, intricate leaves, my other palm cupping the cool marble base. He'd even remembered my love of nature. This man's kindness was such an antithesis to his pampered lifestyle.

"It's beautiful," I breathed, still touching the candelabra.

"I know Hanukkah's over this year, but I wanted you to have the opportunity to light your own candles each night, next year. There are a couple of dreidels in the bag. You'll have to get your own chocolate, though."

I set the heavy gift on my table and threw my arms around Jake's neck. His larger hands cupped my hips as he pulled me closer.

"Thank you. That was so sweet."

"You'll be able to have your own dreidel party next year."

I kissed him then pulled away, heading into the kitchen. "Want anything?"

I needed the moment to compose my thoughts—ones I didn't know how to explain to him.

My parents would never have a dreidel party with me. Once they moved to Tucson mere weeks after my wedding, they'd let me know they were leading their life, their way, finally. That was my mother's parting word to me: *finally.*

"Now that I know about your Fiji obsession, I'd love to take you on holiday." He waggled his brows, eyes smoldering as his gaze dropped to my chest. "You in a bikini, covered in sunscreen. Blimey, that'll be a sight."

I forced a smile as I grabbed a seltzer. With leaden feet, I managed to make it back to the living room and sit beside him on the couch.

"So, tomorrow's the big day," I said, scrambling to say something to move the conversation away from my depressing thoughts. "I hope the practice sessions have been enough."

"You sing for hours each day and you know these songs better than most performers. You'll like the studio. Asher's dying to meet you. Just about took my head off when I told him you couldn't come in till your classes ended. And now I get to spend all day with you, too."

He leaned in and kissed me, and just like that, my worries vanished.

Because kissing Jake took all my focus. My body heated and relaxed, ready to respond to his next move.

Jake didn't disappoint.

But then, he never did. Jake proved to be as thoughtful as he was cautious. He worried over my feelings more than I did.

How could he be so perfect in every way…except with my heart's greatest desire?

I gawked at the space, trying to take in the expensive microphones and full wall of computers and mixing boards on the other side of the plexiglass cage. Soft purple lights glowed in the space on this side of the clear wall, bouncing off the exposed brick and the gleaming hardwood floors. Three stools and as many music stands were set up in front of the big, silver mics. A variety of guitars flanked the maple walls, some of them worth four or five times as much as the pricey guitar Jake and Murphy insisted I keep.

I still felt wrong about that. Never one to mooch, I'd profited from my association with Jake much more than he did from knowing me. Sure, he was staying with me, sleeping with me. For the moment, at least.

I glanced away, worried Jake would notice the unhappiness that crept upon me whenever Jake and I weren't touching. Maybe it was withdrawal from no longer seeing the kids in my classes every day. Some had moved on to the next program, and I'd miss them—they were the original babies from my first classes, and many of their parents had become my friends. Didn't help that I hadn't talked to Linda in a couple of weeks. She'd gone back to Wisconsin to visit her ailing mother. I did talk to my mother again a few days ago, when she called to ask why I hadn't mentioned my "someone" was Jake Etsam. This time, I was the one too busy to talk to her.

"You 'right?" Jake asked, his hand landing on my lower back.

"Not sure." I sounded like Kermit the Frog with a bad case of laryngitis. "Nervous."

The rest of this week was devoted to recording the other three lullabies Jake and I agreed on together. We'd decided to sing "All the Pretty Little Horses" a cappella, no simple feat, but one I thought we'd be able to pull off with Asher's guidance.

I pressed a hand to my stomach, thrilled and terrified to meet the greatest indie rock legend of my lifetime—and my city.

"You're Ryn?" he asked from behind.

I whirled, eyes wide as I stared at Asher Smith. Inside, I was jumping up and down like a fifteen-year-old who'd just been asked out by the school's star quarterback. Outwardly, I smiled and offered my hand.

"I am. It's a pleasure to meet you. In person. I love your music."

Jake chuckled at my gushing ramble, which finally got me to close my mouth. Though Asher's smile nearly had my chin dropping back open. He was *that* potent.

"I love your voice. We've all listened to 'A Moonlit Serenade' this past month. Definitely gave us a high bar to reach. It's going to make this album a success."

Asher Smith just complimented me. My cheeks flushed and I couldn't help the smile that beamed across my face. Jake tightened his arm around me and I glanced over at him, shocked by the pride and possessiveness in his eyes.

"Murphy stopped by last week before he left, trying to snoop around," Asher said. "He's becoming a real pain in the ass."

"What did you tell him?" Jake asked.

"That he hadn't booked any time." Asher's smile built and his eyes sparkled. "And he couldn't because we were booked solid on one of the coolest projects ever for the next month."

"Good thing he's out of town for a few weeks."

Jake and Asher laughed, both looking pleased with their secret.

"You ready to start?" Asher asked, turning back to me. I had to lock my knees to be able to stand my ground. "Jake said you wanted to start with 'All the Pretty Little Horses.'"

"Is that okay?" I asked, trying not to fidget.

"Sure. Just let me get into the booth and we can start. Drinks in the fridge." He pointed to the sleek dorm-sized fridge in the corner before stepping from the room.

I pressed my hand to my tumbling stomach. "That was intense."

"You did great. No fainting."

"But I still have to sing. In front of Asher Smith."

Jake wrapped his arms around me and tugged me to his chest. "You're a'right. You've totally got this. Any time you're worried, just close your eyes and pretend you're singing to your babies."

My babies. His words caused a lump to form in my throat, but I nodded, mainly because I needed the long moment to compose my now-wet eyes.

"You ready?" Asher asked over the PA. I pulled back from Jake's embrace, and settled on the far-right stool, knowing Jake preferred to be on the left.

I blew out a breath, palm pressed to my fluttery stomach. "Let's do this."

———◆———

Each day, I learned something from Asher and Jake— something that showed me how much I still had to learn about my craft.

The week humbled me, in part because we only made it through "All the Pretty Little Horses."

We'd finished a fourth version of the tune when Asher threw down his headset and stalked out of his booth. My chest fluttered as I waited for him to yell at me. Instead, he turned to Jake.

"Will you stop trying to overpower her voice? Yours doesn't have the same richness. Harmonize like you do with Hayden and Ets, but don't make her harmonize with you. It's killed the vibe."

He turned on his heel, shouting, "We're done for the night!"

I stood, rooted to the spot, shocked by this, the first outburst I'd ever seen from Asher. "Is he *always* that intense?" I whispered.

"He's a freaking genius. Yes," Jake added. "No. This is tame."

"I don't want to mess up your album."

"You're not mucking it up. Didn't you hear Asher? That's on me." Jake scrubbed his palms over his face. "Right-o. Well, we're on holiday now. So, after Christmas, we come back and see what I've managed to fix."

"Is recording always like this?"

Jake's lips flipped up in a smirk. "You should see the fights Hayden and Murphy get into. Those are epic."

"Rather not," I squeaked, the mere idea making blood leave my head.

Jake ushered me from the booth. "Recording is hard. The industry rewards innovation and talent, sure, but it's fueled by emotion. That's what songs are—bits of emotion feeding your brain."

"This is so different from my singing-to-babies world."

"Different but still needs the talent. But we have to figure out how to harness your strengths to mine."

I swallowed hard. "And if we don't?"

Jake's face slid into grim lines. "We blow the deadline and don't get the album out."

———•———

After that Monday when Murphy and Mila joined me at one of my music classes, journalists pounced on me anywhere I went. The questions ranged from mundane: "What's your favorite Jackaroo song?" to the insane: "Are you and Jake engaged?" Yesterday morning while Jake was at a nearby gym with Alan, I made the mistake of going online to find a ninety-person chain of Twitter users focused on my stomach. One blogger claimed that since Jake moved in with me a few days ago, I must be pregnant with the next Etsam prodigy.

That one comment devastated me, and I'd locked myself in the bathroom and cried in my shower until the water cooled too much to stay.

Jake arrived home sometime during my shower, but I didn't mention my crying jag and neither did he. Sometime in the last few days, I developed a complex between the push-pull in my desire for Jake and a need to protect myself from him.

The speculation would grow even larger as Christmas neared and Jake stayed with me—even though Mila and Murphy had flown back to Sydney to visit Jake and Murphy's mother, Susan.

"We'll have to go visit soon. Mum's terrified of planes and isn't over the last flight. I took her home on a private charter after she came to ream out Murphy."

I glanced over, my coffee cup halfway to my mouth. "She did what?"

"Murphy was out of control, so Mum flew to Seattle and boxed his ears. After hugging him first, of course."

"Of course." My tone turned dry, but Jake talked with or texted his mom a few times a week—their relationship showed a much tighter family dynamic than mine with my parents. I spoke with Joyce a couple of times since Jake and I started dating, but refused her offer to visit for the holidays—just as I'd refused her offer for dinner last week.

"My mum's talked my ear off about you. I've never stayed with a woman, and she can't get over how pretty you are in the photos she's seen. I half believe she thinks I pay you to be with me."

"Your mom thinks I'm a call girl?" I asked, appalled.

"No," Jake said, eyes wide. "Blimey. No! She can't believe someone as talented and beautiful as you spends time—shares her home—with me. That's what I meant."

"So, she thinks I'm a snob?"

"Zipping my lips. I've stepped in it, and I'm not digging this hole deeper."

He stuttered the last few words, and my heart melted. This man who worked so hard at projecting a confident front was as concerned about my rejection as I was his inevitable one of me.

"Next year, we'll go to Oz for Chrissie. That way we can build some new traditions together. Unless you want to visit your family."

"You've heard me talk to mine," I said on a sigh. "They're not interested in much outside their own enjoyment these days." Which didn't involve me.

Jake settled onto the couch and pulled me down so I straddled him. I wound my arms around his neck because that's where they belonged.

"Your parents' loss, then, because I want you with me." He leaned up and kissed me, a soft, gentle kiss asking for more.

His kisses always worked. "All right. But on one condition."

Jake nodded, eyebrows raised.

"You asked me what I wanted most in the world. What do you want?"

He ran his hands from my waist and over my hips. "Beside you in my bed? Can't believe I'm lucky enough for that one."

My stomach ached at his words. I wanted him to want *me*,

not just my body and the amazing orgasms we shared. We did have more than that—at least some of the time. Jake craved affection as much as I did; he liked to snuggle or hold hands, to kiss me and just be near, even if we were both engrossed in separate activities.

Living with Jake proved easier than I'd expected. Dez, an amazing cook and back-rub specialist, lived in a mess—his clothes piled wherever he took them off, and he never managed to get his dirty dishes in the sink, let alone in the dishwasher to clean. Jake, however, did most of those chores without thought or prompting.

And that scared me, too, because he had slid into my life with such ease. That had to prove…something.

Christmas morning dawned cool and overcast. I yawned my way to the kitchen where Jake brewed a peppermint mocha. I wrapped my arms around his waist and hugged him hard. Jake turned around and kissed me, hungry for each nuance of my lips and tongue against his. He pulled back, eyes heavy, and shifted me a little to ease the pressure in his groin.

"Happy Christmas, Lauryn," he said, brushing my hair off my cheek as he handed me a steaming red mug. "Ready to open your prezzie?"

"What?" Goodness, the drink smelled divine. Might be Jake's fancy new high-end coffee maker. Or the fact he bought the expensive coffee beans that never quite fit into my budget. I took a sip and moaned.

"Nope, no distractions. Presents. You know, the traditional exchange of gifts."

"I-I know what it is. But you already got me a menorah."

He kissed the end of my nose. "For Hanukkah. This is for

Christmas."

He darted into the living room and pulled out a bulky, silver-wrapped present from behind the small Douglas fir we'd picked out and decorated last week in between recording sessions. I walked over and handed him his mug, head tipped to the side.

"I love giving prezzies," Jake said with a smile. "One of my favorite things, really."

Which reminded me. "You never told me."

"Told you what? That was out of nowhere." Jake set the present on the wooden coffee table and accepted the mug, sipping deep.

"What you want most."

His eyes widened. "Did so. You."

I shook my head and gripped my mug, trying to prevent the shivers racing over my spine. "I won't give you your present until you tell me."

A thick red flush heated Jake's cheeks and turned his ears red. He cleared his throat and glanced at me from the side of his eye. "To get my master's, maybe a PhD in art history. I've put in an application at Northern."

"That's what you were looking at between my classes? The art department?"

"Yeah."

I set my mug on the end table and laid my hands on his shoulders. "Really?"

His eyes darted to the package on the table and back to mine, before he drank deep from his mug. "I love art."

"More than music?"

"Dunno if *more* is that right word. I planned to run a

museum or a gallery one day. Now…" he settled the mug in his lap and fiddled with the handle. "If I…if I was being totally honest with you, I'd like to work on my degree and help with your music classes sometimes. Record this album, maybe another next year. But at a slower, more manageable pace that would leave me time to pursue owning a gallery for young, new artists—give them a shot at fame and a good living. And…and spend every night in bed with you." He raised his eyes to mine and held me gaze. He sucked in a deep breath, his words thick as he said, "That's what I want most."

This poleaxe to my chest, the fresh slice of Jake's obvious desire for me, left me speechless.

Because he gave me my deepest need: Acceptance. Caring. Which meant I might never get the child I craved because I couldn't ask him to go against *his* greatest need.

CHAPTER SIXTEEN
Jake

I picked up the gift-wrapped box and handed it to Ryn as my heart stuttered in my chest. Baring my soul to her moments ago, telling her how I'd like my life to progress, made me second guess this choice.

Before I could snatch it from her hand and throw it in the rubbish bin, Ryn settled onto the sofa and turned the package over. She slit the tape and unwrapped the box as my heart rate ramped up further.

The painting wasn't large—sixteen by twenty—but the artist used a striking palette in that limited space. I'd never given much thought to the Pacific Island landscape until I stumbled across this artist, who'd set up shop in Seattle just two months ago. The texture caught and held my attention, and based on Ryn's widened eyes and stuttered breath, she also engaged with the piece.

My shoulders eased as I drank the last of my coffee. Right. Good. Not the bust I feared.

She turned it over, her swallow audible in the quiet room. "Is this…Jake, is this an *original*?"

"Yeah."

"You bought me an original piece of art?"

"It's Fiji," I said. "See the frangipani?"

"I do," she breathed, her fingertips hovering over the hot-pink dollops of oil paint.

"Can't take you to the island right now so I brought the island to you."

With great care, and shaking hands, Ryn set the painting on

the coffee table. My turn to swallow as dryness coated my throat.

"If you don't like…"

Ryn threw herself into my arms. "I love it! Oh, my word! It's the most amazing gift I've ever received."

"You sure? Because I can always—"

She placed her fingers over my lips. "Stop. Don't say it. I love the painting."

"The artist's local. She's part of the reason I want to open the gallery. So I can showcase talent like hers. She's bloody brilliant. Her landscapes are some of the most detailed I've seen outside of museums."

Ryn sat back and smiled at me but it held puzzlement.

"What?"

"You," she said. "I think you mean it. The gallery, your degree, spending time with…with me."

"Course I do." I cupped her cheek and forced my jaw to relax so I could give her the words. Words I hoped she'd give back. "You matter to me. So damn much."

Her eyes slid close, highlighting her lashes on her cheeks as she smiled. "Thank you for that. And the painting." She pressed a kiss to my palm, and my breath caught at the softness of her lips, the emotions in her eyes as she met my gaze.

Blimey, I was in deep with this woman. I'd have to talk to Murphy—see if these emotions swirling through me were what he felt for Mila.

I wanted to make her happy. Not just content, but so bloody happy she couldn't help but smile and laugh—I loved her laugh.

I thought I might love her, too.

I stood and grabbed our mugs. "Another cuppa? Then we can

hang the painting?" I headed into the kitchen. "Any idea where you want it?"

"Somewhere I can see it every day."

I smiled at her response as I refilled the machine.

She stepped into the kitchen and handed me an envelope.

"It's not a painting, but…" Her smile turned down as concern filled her eyes. "Alan said you hadn't been yet."

I caged her with my arms. "You didn't have to get me anything," I said, nuzzling into her neck.

"You are difficult to buy for. Mm. I like that."

I pressed another open-mouthed kiss to her neck and then plucked the envelope from her hand. I opened the seal and pulled out the tickets—four of them—to the Andrew Wyeth exhibition at the Seattle Art Museum.

Excitement bubbled up from my stomach, filling my chest. Andrew Wyeth. Blimey. I'd wanted to see his work up close for years. "You're serious? You got me tickets to this?"

She nodded. "We're going tomorrow. If that's okay? I got tickets for Alan and Isaac, too."

My lips covered hers, and I moaned as I drew her closer. Besides Betsy, no woman had ever entertained my love of art, my desire to wander through a museum for hours on end, as anything other than a silly past time.

"I bloody love it! And tomorrow, you say? I can't wait. I need to read up again on Wyeth's biography, know what to look for."

Ryn pulled another present from behind her back and handed it to me. Inside was a book of Wyeth's painting, his history, and his contemporaries.

I stood in the kitchen, flipping through the book, happier

than I'd been in years. Maybe ever.

Because of Ryn. She made herself another cuppa and leaned against the counter, eyeing me over the rim of her mug. I turned the book toward her, showing her the large painting of a family gathered at a festive dinner.

"Might be their Chrissie. Mine's better."

She smiled, and her gaze held amusement, but something else: that sadness I'd seen the first day I met her when she held the bub in her arms.

Ryn hadn't brought up the topic since I told her my hang-ups, but yearning poured off her, still. Perhaps because today was time for family, for traditions and laughter and togetherness, and it was just the two of us. Maybe she missed Dez and his family and the memories they'd built together.

I clenched my fists around the book and considered my options. I wasn't stupid enough to think Ryn would stick by me forever. A child was too important to her, and I had to respect that need. Just as she'd respected my desire to see what we built together by picking up birth control pills.

I'd talk to her—when she brought it up next. Because I wanted Ryn. Bad. For longer than this time we worked on the album. Couldn't blame the eggnog for this yearning burrowing into my soul.

Ryn, her messy past, her oddly perfect job, her inability to meet a daily baby-cuddle quota, her willingness to not just humor my love of art but actively participate by going to museums with me—she'd become my life.

Now all I had to do was tackle my deepest fear to ensure she got what she needed, which would ensure I got what I couldn't live without.

CHAPTER SEVENTEEN
Ryn

I held the note, using my stomach muscles to clear the air from my diaphragm. My gaze focused not on the microphone in front of me, but on Asher's beaming face through the plexiglass. He made the cut sign, and I let the note fade.

"And that's a wrap!" Asher laughed, his white teeth flashing that perfect smile, as he hopped up from the booth. I pinched the inside of my wrist, just to make double-sure these past six weeks I'd been working with Asher and Jake weren't some crazy dream.

Jake whooped, pulling me into his arms from the wooden stool as he spun me around the studio space, so giddy with the high of that take that we nearly slammed into the guitars on the far wall.

"Jake," I chided, but I was laughing. The joy of a fantastic studio session had me as excited as Jake and Asher.

I'd spent the week after Christmas and early morning and evening hours throughout January singing and playing the guitar and piano for Asher Smith. *And he loved my work.*

I wasn't making that up. He'd told me every day I was here, awe resounding from his voice. "You have range. Good golly, girl, but you can sing!"

"Better than Preslee's," Jake averred again.

"Her rendition of 'Des Colores' brought tears to my eyes," Asher said, shaking his head. "We work with some talented people." He'd turned his gaze to me, eyes narrowed into a squint he normally saved for serious conversations. "We're getting 'A Moonlit Serenade' down today. Long as it takes."

I nodded, palm pressed to my belly as I tried to ease the butterflies building there.

Mere hours later, we celebrated the specialness of this track. Everything flowed. Jake and I were in sync, and the emotion— my desire to make and love a child with Jake, a feeling I couldn't articulate to him directly—poured into every nuance of my voice.

"That was amazing." I kept my arms around Jake's neck, needing him to ease the ache in my chest and womb.

Jake pressed a soft, sweet kiss to my lips, his hands cradling my body to his chest. "You lit it up, love." The pride in his voice warmed the coldness inside enough for me to let go and step back in time for Asher to slap Jake's shoulder.

"Mila's going to love this version. It's even better than the MP3 her friend gave her. Blimey, that's a lovely lullaby. Gonna make the bubs slide into sleep."

Why did Jake have to say that? And with such pride beaming on his face. Pride in me—even though he hadn't once mentioned our living arrangement—heck, us seeing each other again—since Christmas. Granted, the last few weeks of hectic of work with additional three days a week added to the rehearsals and studio time didn't leave much down time. Most nights, Jake and I fell into bed, late, but always in a tangle of limbs that led to heated caresses, followed by five or six hours of sleep. I wasn't sure how we'd managed the schedule, but I couldn't miss a minute of my time with Jake.

The record's deadline loomed closer with each day, and without further reassurances, without words of love I craved, I worried Jake had changed his mind. That while he liked me and enjoyed my body, he planned to leave me as soon as the record was complete.

Irrational though the fear was, it grew the closer we got to this point. I ached more than I had moments ago when I poured all my yearning into the song. Because now…now that the album was complete, Jake had no reason to stay.

"No mixing," Asher said, rubbing his hands together. "What you did there—that was amazing. I'm blown away."

He hugged me, lifting me off the ground. "I'll write a song for us to sing together. Damn, I cannot wait to have you on my next album."

Asher's fame, like Jake's, was world-renowned. If the sales projections Asher and Jake spoke of came to fruition, my bank account would see a couple of zeroes in the right place.

And if I sang with Asher—if that single sped up the charts like most of his songs do—I'd be able to afford not just one of the guitars like the one Murphy gave me, but anything else I could think of.

My throat clogged as if it couldn't decide which emotion to push through next.

Jake and Asher went into the sound booth and listened to the song again while I straightened the studio. Done there, I collected my coat and waited by the door while my emotions continued to battle for supremacy.

"Now that this tune is locked down, we're ready to roll it out. Full length digital goes up on February eleventh. A full day early, man!" Asher said, beaming. "If you're ready, we can start the promo now that this is in the can. We can release a single tomorrow afternoon, pick up some preorders. When are you planning to give it to Mila?"

"I'll drop by their place tomorrow first thing. I'll give them the vinyl copy for their wedding gift."

My jaw dropped. Within the week, the album would be live.

Asher yawned, covering his mouth and shaking his head. "I'll let you know if we run into anything last minute, Jake. Great working with you both."

He shook Jake's hand before pulling him into a hug. Then, he hugged me one more time before he strolled back to the booth and started shutting down his equipment.

"Tired?" Jake asked.

I kept my eyes downcast as I nodded. I was tired, but not in the way Jake thought.

I didn't want to lose him—after tonight there wasn't a reason for him to stay. And he didn't understand my fixation with my own family, which was my fault because I'd never fully explained.

He'd never met my parents. Never seen the lack of love in their eyes. Never known how hard I worked to get a "we expect more from you" response—if I received any notice at all.

I didn't want him to know my parents barely tolerated me. When I told him, he'd leave. Just like they did. Just like Dez. And I'd be alone again.

I hated being alone.

"You're quiet," Jake said, clasping my hand as we exited the restaurant the next night. I wore my blue cashmere dress—I knew Jake liked it—and my black heeled boots. I'd hoped the outfit would boost my sagging confidence. Give me a reason to tell Jake my fears and needs, especially now that the spread in the local paper came out this morning. A variety of pictures of us, together, from the past two months peppered the large article, along with Jake's comments about sticking around Seattle to spend more time with "the people important to him." The article hinted at marriage, but neither Jake nor I had discussed the next phase of our relationship. How could I? I was still reeling from my revelation around Christmas that Jake mattered more to me than the child I'd always dreamed of.

Walking toward the car, a flash of red splashed across my face, and I closed my eyes with a squeak, turning my head against further threats.

"Oi!" Jake yelled.

I sputtered then finally gagged and spat out the remnants of the liquid from my mouth.

Feet pattered past me, but my eyes dripped with whatever covered my face.

"You all right?" Jake asked, his voice solicitous but an undercurrent of fury settled there. I gagged again and began to shiver in earnest as the liquid soaked through my coat and dress.

"What is it?"

"Paint. Red paint." Jake spat. "Isaac ran after the person."

"Oh."

"I'm calling the police."

"What? No! I'm fine."

"I'm bloody well not."

I looked him over, noting the red on his slacks and shoes. "I'm so sorry! I'll pay for new ones." I shook my hands, trying to get some of the wet, sticky substance off me. I wanted to wipe my face. After glancing down at my ruined coat, I used the paint-free sleeve to clear my eyes and mouth.

Jake pulled his phone from his pocket, the scowl building as he glared at Isaac, who jogged back toward us, shaking his head.

"Don't." I grabbed his hand, fingers gripping his tight. "Please."

"Why not? You were accosted."

"By Sam," I said on a sigh, my stomach plunging at my words. Where had our relationship gone so wrong? My knees weakened and I wanted to collapse but managed not to. "I'm pretty certain I saw her. Before she threw the paint."

"You sure it was her?"

I pulled at my paint-covered hair, considering the question. No, not one hundred percent. But I nodded. "I'll call her parents when I get home."

Jake continued to scowl. "Don't like this. She's a menace, maybe more."

I raised my hand to place it on his chest, but thought better of it when red dripped from my wrist to the ground. "Please."

He glanced around, annoyance making his nostrils flare before he shook his head, eyes dropping back to mine. "Let's get you home."

"I'm not sitting in your new car all covered in paint!"

"Neither my car nor my clothes matter near as much as your safety, Ryn. Please don't fight me on this. I *need* to help you."

Why did his words tug at my heart? Why did he have to say such sweet things to me? Words that kept me confused and so in love I craved him more than my next breath.

He tugged me even closer and kissed me, paint and all. Just like every other time, I leaned into the kiss, desperate for more of this feeling Jake created in me, craving his touch, forgetting everything else. Even how cold I was in my wet, ruined clothes.

"I bloody well care about you, Lauryn. More than I should, maybe. I can't stop even though you're still caught up in your ex's family." He dropped his forehead to mine. "I don't want to stop caring for you. Just...just don't ask it of me."

His fingers speared into my sodden hair as he ravaged my mouth. His tongue stroked mine until I tangled mine with his. He growled and upped his assault, plastering me against his chest, bracketing my hips with his thighs. He made love to my mouth with an urgency I couldn't resist and I fell, harder and farther than before, into Jake Etsam.

I stared up into his eyes, seeking an answer he couldn't yet give me—maybe never would. But passion and fury lit his gaze, and I shivered again, this time from the knowledge that Jake was in my blood as well as my mind—any attempt to disengage from him would tear me apart.

"Come on. Since you won't let me call the police, let's get you home and cleaned up."

Isaac kept a pace behind us, frustration rolling off him in a thick wave.

I remained quiet as Jake led me to his car. I insisted on removing my coat so I wouldn't get more paint on his seat. I pulled up the loose ends of my soaked hair into a messy knot on the top of my head, I managed to buckle in without smearing much paint on his leather interior.

Jake removed his coat and button-down shirt, which he laid over his paint-stained trousers. Twenty minutes later, he pulled into a spot in my building and we managed to gingerly exit the car, Isaac popping out of his vehicle parked to my right.

"We're headed up," Jake said to Isaac.

He nodded, eyes moving around the garage. "Want me to go with you?"

"No. We're fine," Jake replied. I sighed with relief at the single red smear on Jake's steering wheel. As we headed toward the elevators, I balled up my ruined coat.

"Tonight didn't go as planned."

Jake pressed the button for my floor as he gave me the side eye. "Not hardly. But you do look good as a redhead."

I threw my head back and laughed, releasing the tension that had built inside me over the past month of intensity. Jake smirked back.

The doors opened we headed down the hallway. Thankfully, no one was out to see our bedraggled appearance. I pulled out my keys, fumbling with the crusty clasp. Jake cursed, low and vicious.

A picture of Dez was taped to my door. He was in full dress uniform, his hair recently shorn in the military buzz cut. He looked so young and full of life.

Beneath the picture, in the same red paint that covered me, the words read, "*Until death do you BOTH part.*"

I dropped my keys, hands covering my mouth.

Jake reached into his pocket and yanked out his phone. "This is an escalation. We can't ignore this. And I won't, not even for your crazy, over-the-top loyalty to people who treat you so poorly."

I nodded, my chest hollow as I stared at the words—and the implicit promise of them.

CHAPTER EIGHTEEN
Jake

I photographed the picture and note before I let Ryn into her apartment. Maybe not the wisest choice, but she was shivering and making these strange gasping sounds, barely able to stand. I called Detective Davenport on his cell as soon as we were inside and I'd locked the door, speaking in a low voice so as not to freak Ryn out further. After telling us not to change or shower, he promised to bring a police photographer with him and hung up.

An hour and a half later, Ryn and I huddled on her sofa, our clothes shedding bits of dried paint. Ryn insisted on making me a cuppa tea when we came in, but those mugs, left untouched, sat in front of us on the coffee table, long-cold.

"I don't have the full picture," Detective Davenport said, leaning forward so his elbows rested on his knees. "Explain to me your relationship with your deceased husband's family."

Ryn's body stiffened and I caught her glance at me. Did she want me to leave? Was she still in love with him? Blimey, that thought hurt enough that I rubbed my chest before I realized how obvious I was being.

I cared for Ryn—deeply—but I wasn't sure what love was, really. Not like my parents were the best examples of the emotion.

Murphy's extreme focus on Mila, her well-being, making sure she was happy and safe, came much closer to my own feelings for Ryn—along with fear and impotent rage each time she called Ted or Joyce.

I'd thought living together for a while would clarify my feelings. A trial run for what we'd do if our relationship progressed further.

I never told Ryn I bought a two-bedroom flat the day I moved out of the suite—in her building, on her floor—for my body guards. She thought I'd rented the place—by sheer luck. I hadn't said more about the apartment because I wanted to spend all my time with Ryn. She seemed to like having me around, and I made a point of keeping up with the laundry and house cleaning—both chores I used to do for my mum. Ryn never asked me to do anything, and surprise and thankfulness lit up her face whenever I helped, making me wonder even more about her relationship with Dez.

Ryn twisted her fingers, a sure sign of her discomfort. Unable to watch her tug at the skin, causing it to go white, I placed my hand over hers.

"My parents didn't want me."

Her words were quiet, but firm in their truth, and they broke my heart. I squeezed her cold fingers, but she didn't respond to my gesture.

"Excuse me?" Detective Davenport said.

"They didn't want me. I was a late-in-life surprise. My father turned fifty the week after my birth. They'd been itinerant up until that point—traveling the world with no clear purpose. He insisted on opening an insurance company, and my mother worked for him. They worked a lot. So I spent time at the neighbor's. At Dez and Sam's."

"I'm still unclear as to why you think your parents didn't want you." Davenport's voice was kindly but the words were not.

Ryn's hand convulsed beneath mine. "They told me I was a mistake. That's one of the first conversations I remember."

"That's why you don't call them often," I said.

She kept her head bowed, as if she feared seeing my reaction, but she whispered, "Yes."

"So, you spent time at the neighbors' house," Detective Davenport said, his voice gentle. His face held the kind of sympathy Ryn deserved but would never accept.

"Pretty much *all* my time because I was friends with Dez and Sam. My parents appreciated the ease as my relationship developed with Dez. Joyce and Ted accepted me as their own long before Dez proposed."

Ryn and the detective continued to talk, but my mind spun out in myriad thoughts: Ryn's expression every time I said I wasn't ready to start a family, the sad longing with which she stared at the children in her classes, the sobs she didn't think I heard when she stayed in the shower for an hour, the pack of birth control pills that sat on the bathroom counter, each day another pill missing, and her slow pull back from me the closer we came to the completing the album.

My dad hurt my family—destroyed it, some would say—whereas Ryn's parents took away her sense of safety and ability to belong. She searched for it, desperate for the connection, just as I tried to escape any opportunity that could lead me down my father's path.

My hand still covered hers, the smears of cracked red paint—the gulf widening between the edges just as my fear caused a deepening chasm between Ryn and I. One I hadn't seen because I didn't want to.

Her fingers were long and slender, her nails short and neat, covered in a pale-pink polish. Strong hands, capable ones. But her voice—the hoarseness that showcased the pain she'd buried for years—bit into my chest, leaving it open and bleeding.

To give me the space and lack of responsibility I wanted, Ryn began to forfeit her own desires and happiness. And I'd accepted her doing so as my due. Hell, my *right* for staying with her, invading her home and bringing unwanted media scrutiny and further stress.

Ryn's hand kept trembling but she straightened her spine.

Dez, Sam, Joyce, Tim, the kids in her program, even Asher and me…we took from her. Took parts of Ryn. Because she let us.

Ryn disappeared as soon as the detective left. The water turned on, and, only after I was sure she was under the water, I tested the door handle, unsurprised but disappointed she'd locked the door. Didn't even break me off my game—I collected the thinnest of Ryn's knitting needles and popped the lock in seconds.

After stripping my clothes, I opened the shower curtain. Ryn, her back to the shower's spray, tipped her head back toward the water, red streaming from her long hair into the drain. Her neck arched, pushing up her wet, luscious breasts. Blimey, I was a lucky, lucky man.

I stepped into the tub just as Ryn opened her eyes and met my gaze. Her eyes held a pain too deep-seated to ever annihilate.

"Why didn't you tell me?" I asked, my voice gravelly with emotion. One of which, I was shocked to realize, was anger.

She dropped her gaze and wrapped those wet arms around her middle. "Because then you'd leave, too. Everyone does eventually."

"That's a fucking long leap for you to make. I'm not your parents. I'm *not* Dez. And I don't like the comparisons." Before she had time to take a breath, my mouth covered hers. My lips ravaged hers over and over, seeking entrance into the warm cavern of her mouth, going deeper each time, proving my point that she was mine…and in doing so, I was hers.

She mewled into my mouth, her fingernails scrabbling for purchase on my wet shoulders. I pressed her tighter against the tiles, lifting her right leg as I thrust my hips into her welcoming heat. I pulled back long enough to catch a breath, the groan ripping from my throat as I swiveled my hips. I wanted to tell her I'd become certain of one important truth as she spoke with Detective Davenport: I was in profound, acute love with her. The words hovered on my lips, but when Ryn tipped her head back with a gasp as I hit that spot she loved, my mouth drifted to her neck, licking and nibbling my way back up to her lips— the ones I craved.

Long after the shudders from pleasure wracked our bodies, long after I helped Ryn wash her hair and skin, long after I cuddled her in bed, I lay awake, puzzling through the bits of Ryn's past I knew. Her loyalty and selflessness shown brighter than any beacon.

I climbed out of bed around 1:30 a.m. and grabbed my phone. I closed her bedroom door and turned on the under-cabinet lights in her small kitchen, enjoying the faint, warm glow. Opening a beer, I pulled up my e-mail account and began to type out a series of messages.

Ryn would never ask more of me. Not when unworthiness had been ground into her soul by her bloody awful parents.

Here I was—crying over my shit-bag father when my mum threw the bastard out to ensure Murphy's and my continued safety and happiness. Not only did I have my mum's unwavering love, I had Murphy's and Mila's. But Ryn's "family" consisted of people who insisted she partake in their traditions to become part of their family.

The revelations caused my chest to ache.

Ryn seemed so put together, so capable, so loving. And she was. Yet, I understood about veneer, the façade I wanted the world to see. That kept people from delving to the unhealed scars and tender bits of themselves too fragile for others to know. Ryn lived her entire childhood being told she was a burden—a waste of time and energy.

Combatting that level of neglect and, yeah, abuse, would take time—if she ever healed fully.

I sipped the last of my beer and stared out into the dark, gray fog laying heavy over the city. I should have talked to my mum or even Murphy more about my fears of becoming my father—of how it had twisted inside me. Because in telling Ryn I wouldn't have a child, I forced her into a terrible choice: be with me, or have that unconditional love she didn't just crave, she needed, with the same desperation a seed sought the sun.

CHAPTER NINETEEN
Ryn

The knock on my door early the next morning jolted me from deep slumber. I rubbed my eyes, still gritty from a late night and the intensity of emotions wrung out of me by talking with the police and then, my shower with Jake.

I glanced over to where he lay on his side, facing me. His lips were slightly parted, his cheeks relaxed. His hair flopped forward onto his brow. My handsome man. He'd reconfirmed it for me again last night, not just with his words but with his mouth, tongue and, I blushed hard, the rest of his body.

The rapping at the door started up again. Jake's brows scrunched as he snuggled deeper into the pillow. I jumped from bed, grabbing my robe and tying it over the tank top and flannel pajama pants I'd put on after our shower. I closed the bedroom door firmly, hoping to get rid of whomever it was before they woke Jake.

A quick glance in the peephole caused my heart to hammer and my mouth to dry out.

I opened the door with trepidation. "Ted. Joyce."

"How could you do this to us?" Joyce demanded, storming into my apartment.

I glanced back at the bedroom door, hoping Jake managed to sleep through this altercation. Then I bit my lip, thinking of the promise I'd made him. But these were Dez's parents. They wouldn't hurt me.

Then again, I'd never thought Sam would hurt me either.

"I guess you heard the Seattle police department planned to

bring Sam in for questioning."

"For questioning! The officer handcuffed my daughter and put her in the back of the cruiser not twenty minutes ago!"

I closed my eyes and tilted my head back, hating how Dez's death still caused so much pain.

"You shouldn't have done that, Ryn." Ted's voice was softer than Joyce's, but his calmness made me shiver. "I told you I'd take care of the situation."

"Unfortunately, Sam escalated the situation to a point I couldn't wait for you to 'take care of it.'" I walked toward my small kitchen—eyeing the counter where I'd left my phone. Jake, ever thoughtful, had plugged it into the charger. "You woke me. I need some coffee. Either of you want some?"

Joyce made a strangled sound while Ted followed me. So much for texting Jake or even Linda with ease. But I did slip my phone into my pocket before I began the task of filling the coffeemaker.

I set out mugs and turned, bumping into Ted, who frowned down at me. For the first time in my life, Ted intimidated me. His eyes held daggers, all pointed at me.

My phone buzzed in my pocket, and I bit back a scream.

No reason for this jumpy feeling. These were my in-laws. People I'd known my whole life—I'd spent nearly as many nights at their house as my own, growing up. They wouldn't hurt me.

With a shaking hand, I managed to pour a cup of coffee. I shoved it at Ted's chest and pulled out my phone at the same time, sidestepping around him. Caffeine could wait—my adrenaline level shot up to highest alert.

The text was from Alan. *You okay with your company?*

Thank goodness Alan and Isaac had a place in the building, and one of them always remained on duty. I texted him back: *In-laws just showed up. Not happy with me.*

I hit "Send."

Joyce paced around my living room while Ted set his coffee on my counter, arms crossed and scowl building to new, darker heights.

I pocketed my phone and tried to rearrange my features into a pleasant expression.

"I hope you know I don't have any ill will against Sam. She's just stuck in her grief."

"Unlike you." Ted's anger slid over me, leaving me cold and even more afraid.

Jake's words from one of our late-night pillow talks came back to me: *Mila thought she could handle her stalker herself. That cost her and Murph their unborn child and nearly got her killed. I don't want to run your life for you, make all your decisions. But I do want you to be safe. And I can help you with that. Let me, Ryn, Please.*

My phone chimed again.

"Will you turn that damn thing off? For God's sakes, we deserve your full attention!" Joyce said, advancing into my space.

"Yes, of course. Let me tell Linda I'll have to meet her later."

I didn't read this message. Just quickly shot off another text: *Scared.*

I shoved my phone back into my pocket but continued to clutch it in my hand. Like a lifeline. I refused to look toward my door, concerned Ted would notice my preoccupation.

"You have my attention."

"Too bad Dez didn't. You were supposed to love Dez forever.

You promised." Joyce's eyes were wet, tear-tracks lined her cheeks.

"I did. And I meant it."

"But look at you. You're all snuggled up to a new man." She spat the word. "Because being married to a *real* hero, a soldier, wasn't enough. You wanted more fame. More, more, more!"

"That's not true nor is it fair," I said, trying to keep my voice calm. But her accusations hurt. Deeply, if I was honest.

Joyce's lip trembled and more tears splashed down onto her cheeks. "It *is*. You've only ever thought about yourself. *You* wanted to get married. *You* wanted your career. Did you ever stop to think about Dez's needs? Ever?"

I clenched my hands together in fists. "Look, I loved Dez. But he had to have things his way—and one of those things was going to basic training and then Lewis-McChord without me. Th-that's why I wanted a baby. I wanted a piece of him." I firmed my chin. "I wanted a piece of him to keep, always, because he wouldn't let me have him." But there was more there. What was it?

"You're lying," Ted said, pulling me away from the realization teasing through my head.

"I'd never lie about my relationship with Desden. I never have. But you need to understand he wasn't perfect."

"Don't speak that way about my boy. My dead boy." Joyce wrapped her arms around her waist.

"I know you miss him." I laid my hand on her shoulder. "I do, too."

"Bullshit!" She knocked my hand off, her face twisting in rage. "You wanted your music career, and now you have that. A big star! You're selfish—you've always been a selfish girl, and I wish you'd died instead."

189

I reeled back, my chest aching as I tried to comprehend her words. A fist hammered against the door. Alan, no doubt.

"Joyce," Ted said, his hang-dog eyes flicking to the door. "That's enough."

"It's not!" She turned to glare at me. "Everything was *always* about you! I should have hit you with Sam's car. You deserve that for taking away my son."

I stumbled back into the wall, palms flat, as I stared at Joyce.

"You-you knew, didn't you?" I asked Ted.

"Ryn!" Alan yelled through the door. "Open the door or I'm calling the police."

Ted dropped his chin to his chest, his eyes never leaving my face, his expression blank.

"If Jake didn't pull me back, I might be dead. Paralyzed. And you *covered* for her?" My breath came in small, painful gasps as I backed away. "I never did anything other than love Dez. Ever." Tears leaked down my cheeks and dripped to my chest. My parents might not like me, resented caring for me, but they never actively tried to hurt me. "I loved all of you."

"Time for us to go, Joyce," Ted said, standing up to his full height, his angry, sad eyes boring into mine. "You need to forget what Joyce said here."

"She might," Jake said from behind me. My body melted with relief even as my brain rebelled. Jake heard what Joyce said. What if he agreed with Joyce? What if, even after last night, he left me, too?

"Ryn! Open the door."

I stumbled over to it and managed to turn the handle. Alan barreled into the room, followed closely by Isaac. Both men stepped in front of me, their bodies between me and the threat of my in-laws.

Jake brought his phone forward and pressed play. Joyce's vindictive voice filled the room. *"I should have hit you with Sam's car."*

I shoved my fist against my lips, pressing harder as the sob threatened to overcome me.

"Just so you know, I already forwarded that to my body guards here, brother, and manager. You're not covering this up, mate. Now, we'll let you go because Ryn needs to get away from your wife. But be sure you'll be hearing from my lawyer."

Ted glanced up at Alan, then over to Jake. He dropped his red-rimmed eyes and dipped his head, acknowledging Jake's words.

———◆———

Jake shoved past Alan's big body and pulled me into his arms as Isaac locked the door behind Joyce and Ted.

"Call Detective Davenport, will ya, Alan? Thanks for the ring."

I continued to shiver as Jake led me over to my couch. He hoisted me into his arms and I huddled there, needing the warm safety of his arms and chest.

"Got to tell you, love. I don't like those people."

"They thought…" I swallowed hard, willing back the tears that threatened. "How could they think that of me?"

He brushed my hair off my cheek. "Best guess? Grief. Warped her mind. Just as it did her daughter's."

"You…you were right, Jake. I'm sorry I was angry that you wanted me to contact the police."

And the tears broke free. Tears for the family I'd known and loved, and the man whose death unintentionally broke so many lives.

Jake held me through my tears. He helped me dress and ran a brush through my hair when my hand shook too much to hold the handle. He wrapped his arm around my shoulder, molding me to his side through our official statements and even through my next bout of shaking when I had to make the call as to whether to press formal charges.

"Give us a minute?" Jake asked the detective.

Davenport nodded, his eyes full of sympathy. If we'd met under different circumstances, I would have liked the man much more. Probably considered him the friend Jake did.

"How are you holding up?" Jake asked. I bit my quivering lip but not before Jake saw. He rubbed the back of his neck and turned away.

His reaction caused more tears to push past my rapidly blinking lids—which he turned back just in time to see fall. He gritted his teeth and clenched his fists.

"You gotta let the past go, Ryn."

I wanted to tell him I hated hurting him, hated that he thought my tears fell for Dez or even myself.

"I'll give you a mo'. Me, too. Need to cool off from all this."

And with that, Jake walked out of the room. The sob I'd been holding in burst forth as I heard my front door slam.

"Dammit," I yelled, throwing my pillow across the room. "Dammit!"

"Whoa! I didn't think you cursed."

I turned to see Isaac standing in the doorway of my room, eyes wide.

"I don't, normally. Ever. But I'm…I'm so *fucking pissed* at Dez and his family for hurting Jake." I scrubbed my palms over my wet cheeks. "I need Jake."

"And he needed a breather, which is why he asked me to stay with you."

"You don't have to babysit me. I have Detective Davenport." I waved my hand in the vague direction of my living room.

"I don't mind staying," Isaac said, his voice kind.

"Thank you. But I'm not much for company." I bent down and picked up my pillow. "I appreciate you being here. Really. But go do your thing. I'll touch base once I…" My thoughts turned back to Jake, the frustration on his face. Dread filled my stomach as the worry I'd pushed him away resurfaced.

"I'm not leaving your side, Ryn. Jake asked me to stick here tight, and I mean to do it."

"Did he take Alan with him?" I asked.

Isaac nodded. "Want me to wait in the living room?"

"Please." Once Isaac shut my door, I collapsed back onto my bed, barely listening as Isaac and the detective spoke.

I sat there, head bowed, until Detective Davenport wrapped his knuckles on the edge of my door. "If you need more time to decide what you want to do, that's fine. But we do have a maximum hold period, and if you're not going to press charges, I'll have to let Joyce Hudson go."

I glanced down at my phone, but there was no message from Jake. Not a word from him. My heart tripped then sped up.

I stood fast, my legs wobbly, but determination fierce. I had to finish this. Had to get Joyce, Ted, and Sam out of my life. *Now.*

Jake deserved to know he was all I thought about—that he

was more important to me than the child I might never have. Because while I wanted a baby for more than twenty years of my life, I wanted that child so I wouldn't be alone.

So someone, somewhere, would need me and want me. Love me.

Jake took care of me last night. He did the same this morning. He made sure I was never alone. When he couldn't be here—even if it was because of anger—he made sure I had a companion, a protector. He deserved the same level of care from me.

I could—I would—do this. For Jake but also for myself.

"I'll go to the station with you."

The detective turned on his heel and led me through my apartment, Isaac falling into step beside me after I locked my door.

———◆———

"Why'd you try to hurt me, Joyce?" I had to know.

I sat across the metal table from her, hands folded on top, trying to look composed.

I'd broken down on the way here and texted Jake, letting him know where I'd gone—and why. That was two hours ago, but I still hadn't heard back. Each tick of the clock reverberated through my chest—an omen that I'd lost the man I needed more than my previous dreams.

"Because you needed a wake-up call."

I shook my head, unsure how to respond.

"You think a rock star's going to make you happy? Please. He's shallow. Self-absorbed."

I could tell Ted and Joyce how wrong they were about my

lover. That Jake was much more attuned to my needs than Dez had been—Dez and I had been together so long, on some level we took the other's presence for granted.

I could tell them that Jake was an introvert thrust into an extrovert's role. I could tell them how he read poetry—just last week he read me Maya Angelou's *Caged Bird* as we lay together on the couch. I could tell them how his eyes lit up when we walked through the Seattle Art Museum. How he stopped in front of a particular Wyeth piece and gripped my hand tighter because it stole his breath.

I could tell them he'd started coursework for his PhD, deciding to bypass his master's because he wanted to spend more time with me—and "adding three years more to my education, whilst fun, isn't going to keep you company or all that happy when I'm writing yet another paper."

I could tell Joyce that Jake always put his family's needs before his own—he searched for the perfect house in Murphy's neighborhood in case his mother wanted to spend more time with Murphy and Mila's baby.

I could but I wouldn't. Because those details—Jake's innermost feelings mattered to *me*. I wanted to protect him with the same fierce determination he'd shown for my well-being.

Sam sat at the end of the table, head bowed. She'd appeared an hour earlier with a lawyer for her mother, who sat on the other side of Joyce.

"I'm going to give you a choice. I worked it out already with the district attorney." I didn't tell them that Detective Davenport hadn't liked my plan. More than likely, Jake hated it, too, which was probably why he still hadn't returned my long, rambling text.

"I want all three of you to do a full grief counseling program. I'll help pay the costs out of Dez's life insurance policy. But all three of you must complete the psychologist's full recommended timeframe." I raised my hand to forestall Sam's snappish retort. "If you don't"—I raised my voice to speak over her—"then the charges are reinstated, and the case goes to the grand jury."

I stood up, shoving the chair back. "I'll let you think about it. But you only have…" I looked up at the clock. "You have three hours to decide before Detective Davenport comes back in. He has my and Jake's statements, along with the security cameras that picked up Joyce in my building and at my door, and the closed-circuit camera with Sam's car and license plate. The university's security has images of Joyce entering my classroom."

I tipped my head at Ted, who'd collected that evidence, but hadn't added it to the original report Linda opened for me after my guitar was smashed. Ted dropped his gaze back to the table, understanding he, too, could be charged with obstruction.

I nodded my head once. Only one thing left to say to the family I'd been closer to than my own. "Goodbye."

I exited the room, closing the door behind me. I made it a few feet down the hall before I tipped my head back and closed my eyes, and tried to stop shaking. Someone leaned against the wall next to me. No, not someone. My eyes opened, and I gazed up into Jake's beautiful face. My hand rose to cup his cheek and he turned his face, pressing a kiss against my palm.

"You heard?"

He nodded. "You're a strong woman, Lauryn."

"Not strong enough to tell you how I feel about you."

Jake pressed his fingertip to my lips. "Hold that thought."

"No, Jake, I need to tell you that I lo—"

He kissed me, his tongue thrusting into my mouth with the intent to own me. When he pulled back, my eyes fluttered open, and I stared up into the hard planes of his face, his eyes unfathomable behind his heavy lids.

"Ryn!"

I started, stiffening at Sam's voice. Jake lifted his head to track her progress.

"I'm glad I caught you." She huffed for a minute, her eyes filled with tears. "I needed to tell you I'm sorry. I messed up, not just twenty years of friendship, but Dez's last wish."

Jake stiffened beside me. Before I had time to process how to respond to him, Sam grabbed my hand.

"He loved you. And he told me he should have listened to your wishes about kids. He just always thought you'd have more time together."

Sam's words were freeing. I wished Dez and I had been smarter—and not fallen prey to our parents' expectations—but we'd been young. So sure we had a lifetime together.

Sam looked up at the ceiling, her eyes filling with tears. "I'm sorry for the way I reacted when you met Jake, then at the tree lighting." She wiped away a tear as she smiled.

"You worried about your mom's reaction," I said, the last of the pieces snapping into place. "Because she wanted Dez and me to be forever. Or me mourning Dez forever."

"Yeah." Sam wiped away another tear. "I got scared when she went after you in my car. I thought Dad had her under control after she destroyed your classroom, but…you're right. The grief has eaten away at her. She needs help. We should have gotten it for her. I'll make sure she takes the deal you made for her. And thank you for that." Her voice softened.

Jake remained quiet, at my side. When I looked up, he wore a pensive, almost sad expression. I leaned into his side. "You okay?" I asked.

"Pretty sure I should be asking you that," he said on a sigh.

"I am," I said. Jake met me at the police station, even after I frustrated him this morning. His being here, now, meant everything.

"You seem good for and to her." Sam said, meeting Jake's eyes. "I know...I know it's going to take time for us to be friends again, if we ever can be." Her voice broke as her gaze turned back toward me. "But, I want you to be happy."

Sam pivoted and strode back down the hall toward the conference room I'd exited a few minutes earlier.

I walked forward and pressed the button to the elevator. Jake didn't follow. I glanced back, worry eating its way through my stomach.

When the elevator dinged, Jake charged forward, grabbing my hand on the way. He tugged me into the car and stabbed his finger at the lobby button.

"We're getting out of here."

"Where are we going?" I asked, suspicion building as Jake turned onto I-90 toward Bellevue.

"The airport."

"I can't leave! I'm in the middle of classes."

"Preslee Jennings—Asher's sister-in-law—will cover them for you this week. She's been interested in the classes since she attended the one at the beginning of the semester. Said this would give her the chance to see what you do."

I opened my mouth to argue, irritated at this blatant takeover of my life, my work. Jake laid his hand on top of my fisted ones. "Please, Ryn. I don't do spontaneous well. Ever. But I need to do this with you *now.*"

I snapped my mouth shut, unsure where he was taking me—why he was taking me. The antsy feeling in my chest built. I drew in a deep breath and did something I hadn't in years: I trusted Jake. The only way to ever get past my hang-ups with Dez, to fully embrace a life with Jake—if that was what he wanted—was to believe he'd continue to care about my emotional needs.

He parked the car and came around to open my door. He assisted me out and, still holding my hand, led me toward a sleek, white airplane.

"Private jet?" I asked as he led me up the five steps. "No wonder we didn't go to Sea-Tac."

A flight attendant smiled at us. "Welcome, Mr. Etsam, Ms. Hudson. Your luggage has been stowed and the pilot's been through precheck. Both he and our copilot gave me the thumbs-up once you're settled."

Jake nodded at her, his eyes distant. I trailed behind him as he led me to wide, comfortable seats in the middle of the plane. He motioned for me to choose my seat. I settled into an aisle chair and Jake took the seat next to me.

"Jake, we need to talk."

He took my hand and squeezed it. "We will. When we get there."

"Where's 'there?'"

He rubbed his fingers across his nose. "I don't want to tell you." He stuttered through the words, something I hadn't heard him do in weeks.

Nerves. But what did Jake have to be nervous about?

I bit my lip and looked out the far window.

"Jake, I need to tell you something."

His eyes widened and he swallowed twice. "Please, just wait. This is…I want to do this right."

Something weighty—dread—settled on my chest.

"So we can't talk about Joyce or—"

Jake shook his head once, his hands in fists on his knees. "Maybe you'd like to nap?" he asked, voice hopeful.

I licked my lips, unsure how to respond. Once the plane took off, I asked for a blanket and pillow. The flight attendant suggested I go back to the bedroom.

"There's a bedroom?"

Jake glanced up, still tapping his forefinger against his mouth. "Come on. I'll show you."

I gaped at the size and luxury of the space. I crawled onto the bed and glanced back over my shoulder, trying to make my look as inviting as possible.

"You care to join me?"

Jake's lips flipped up in that insouciant grin I loved so much, but he didn't step into the room. Instead, he shook his head. "Not just yet. I have a couple of calls to make."

I flopped down onto the mattress, frustrated, as Jake closed the door. I rolled to my side, staring at the door, wondering if I should go out there, talk to him against his will. Try to fix whatever I broke between us.

I closed my eyes, willing my mind to function well enough for me to come up with an opener. Why would Jake bring me on a flight if he was angry with me?

My sleep-deprived brain had no answer, and instead, pulled me into a dreamless slumber.

———◆———

I woke later, groggy and uncertain where I was. Jake's arm lay heavy around my waist, his hips spooning mine. I wiggled back against him to enjoy the comfort of his body heat, the soft joy that built each time I snuggled in closer.

Jake's large hand rose, smoothing back my hair.

"How are you feeling?"

I stretched. "Still unclear where we're going."

"If you could go anywhere, where would you want to go?" he asked.

Excitement overrode the concerns I'd fallen asleep with. I turned to face him, eyes wide. "Fiji," I breathed.

Jake dipped his head in affirmation. "Happy Valentine's Day." His brow wrinkled and he shrugged. "A bit early, yet."

"This is by far and away my coolest vacay ever." I threw my arms around his neck. "Thank you."

Jake's eyes darkened and he lowered his head. My skin buzzed in anticipation of this kiss. Afterward, I'd tell him how much I loved him. He'd profess his love for me and this trip would be one of the highlights of my life.

Instead, a sharp, tinny voice spilt through the overhead PA system. "Mr. Etsam, Ms. Hudson, please return to your seats in the main cabin. The pilot is starting his descent."

Jake flung back the covers with a grumble. He pulled on his jeans, buttoning them and then bent down to slip his feet into his shoes. He ran his hands through his hair, tousling the strands into further sexy disarray.

He offered me his hand, but I shook my head. "Go ahead. I'm going to freshen up a little. I'll be quick," I added at Jake's burgeoning frown.

After going to the bathroom and washing my hands and face, I tried to tame my sleep-crazed locks. Frustrated, I ended up pulling the whole mass into a topknot.

I settled into the seat next to Jake, just in time for the actual landing. Jake stopped to thank the pilots as we exited the plane. After a short interval, a Jeep rolled up on the tarmac, and we settled in the backseat.

"You packed us clothes?"

"What?" Jake looked up at me, glancing at the lush scenery. He'd been distracted by whatever was on his phone. "No, I didn't. I called the Neiman Marcus personal shopper Mila uses. She packed us bags of clothes."

"You didn't need to go to that expense," I said on a sigh.

Jake ignored my comment, busy typing a response to the incoming texts that flowed faster than the chiming alert.

After a few minutes, I looked out the window, wishing for some sunglasses against the bright island sun—and to shade my eyes from the tears that refused to blink away.

Jake brought me to paradise. Maybe as his last good deed before he broke up with me? I wrapped my arms around my waist and wished I knew what he was thinking.

CHAPTER TWENTY
Jake

Hours later, I sorted out all the details. Spoke with Murphy, too, finally, just to get his take. I blew out a breath, trying to ease my careening heart. I stepped out onto our private beach as Ryn shifted on her blue-and-white striped chaise, her tanned and toned thigh catching my attention. Blimey, I wanted her. Always would.

"Hiya." I plopped down onto the chaise lounge next to hers. "Enjoying the sun?"

"Yes. Everything okay?"

Her voice held a note I couldn't place. Concern, maybe. I tossed my phone on the chair next to me. "First off, Joyce, Ted, and Sam all took the counseling deal. That was bloody kind of you."

Ryn shrugged, but I caught how she tensed under my continued perusal. Like I could stop looking at her—she was bloody hot in that getup.

"Didn't the album drop today…wait. Yesterday?"

"Yep. Selling hotter than we expected. Over a million so far, last numbers I saw. I knew I was on to something when I heard your voice." I settled on the edge of her chair so I could lean in and kiss her. She responded with the same eager hunger I'd come to expect—her fingers sliding through my hair as she opened her mouth further.

"Mm, I like that," I said, pressing a kiss to the corner of her lip before pulling back. The flash of light off a telephoto lens made me sigh. "Guess the journo did, too. So much for being incognito."

Ryn sighed but continued to rest her palms on my biceps.

This woman. Her strength drew me. Her sexiness drove me crazy. Her voice tantalized me. No way I could ever imagine a life without her.

"We should get back to the hotel if we want to have enough time to shower and get ready."

Ryn raised her eyebrows, her eyes darkening with concern, but she smiled. "Sure."

I helped her up, handing over her sarong. She tied it and slid her feet into her fancy flowered flip flops while I gathered her towel, phone, and water bottle. I grabbed her hand and led her toward our beachfront suite.

Stepping into the room, Ryn's mouth fell open, and she pressed her fingers to her trembling lips as the sweet, light scent of the flowers hit her. I waited, letting her take in the vases of hibiscus, passion plants, and frangipani in every shade of red, pink, and white the hotel staff managed to find.

"Happy Valentine's Day. Er. I know I said that on the plane and sorry it's a little early yet."

She turned to look at me, her eyes wide and glazed with tears. "It's beautiful."

I cupped her cheek. "You're beautiful."

"Jake." She pressed her lips together, her chin trembling. Then she threw herself into my arms, winding her arms tight around my neck, her legs locking behind my back. I grinned, liking where this was going. But first...

"I love you, Lauryn. I love you heaps. Just you *for* you." I kissed her lips. "That's why I planned this trip. I wanted to show you. The first time I said the words needed to be in this place you thought of as magical."

"I love you, too. Ohmygosh. I'm overwhelmed. I can't believe you did all this for me." She fanned her eyes, trying to blink back the emotion welling there.

"That's not the only reason I brought you here. I mean, it was originally. Just to give you a holiday. But, it became more than that once I realized how upset you were about Dez's family."

Her arms loosened and she pulled back, blinking up at me, confusion tugging at her brows. I leaned in and kissed her long and slow and hot enough to leave me panting.

We had a few more items to discuss before I stripped her out of her sarong and swim suit. Just the idea of doing so made my mouth water.

I lowered her feet to the floor, keeping my hands on her hips because I couldn't not touch her. But we needed to sort this out so we could move forward the way I wanted.

"Do you have something you want to tell me?" I asked.

She shook her head, eyes clouded with concern. Much as I wanted to, I didn't let her off the hook just yet.

"About going on birth control?" I prompted.

"Oh." She drew out the word. "Yes, I did. Right after you said the idea of kids freaked you out."

"I know that. I saw the packs on the counter. Want to tell me why?"

She looked down at her bare feet—her toes were painted the same luscious pink as her lips.

"I've heard about women having babies with rock stars. You know, for income. And I didn't want you to think I'd do that to you."

"Never did, love, and you got my context a bit off there. I

said talking to you about bubs when I'd only known you for, like, three days, freaked me out. Which it did."

"But your father…" Her voice trailed away.

"Was a shithead of the highest order. I don't like the man and never will." I closed my eyes and breathed in deeply. "I talked to Murphy and my mum. This is the third convo I've had with them about my dad and genetics."

"O-kay." She drew out the word, clearly uncertain how to respond.

"You never did ask how I got Alan and Isaac into that flat on the same floor as you."

Her brows drew low. "What's that got to do with us?"

I rubbed my thumb across the warm, soft skin of her cheek. "Everything. I bought that place so they'd be near enough for guard duty."

"Why would you do that?"

"They need to be close. And I didn't want to give up my chance to stay with you. I-I've never been in love before, Ryn. With you, I didn't recognize it at first because we just fit. When I did, well, I wasn't sure I could give you what you needed." I threaded my fingers through the hair at her temples, loving the richness of the strands clinging to my fingers. "Why don't you ask me how I feel about having a baby with you now?"

Ryn sucked in a long breath, released it slowly. "How do you feel about having a baby with me, Jake?"

I leaned in and kissed her, bringing my right hand up to cup the back of her head as I pressed my palm flat against the upper swell of her bum so she could feel just how much I liked the idea.

"That's a bloody ripper of an idea. Can't wait."

"Wh-what? But that's so…spontaneous."

"Not as spontaneous as you think. We've been together months now, and I've had time to think on it even before I talked to my mum. She told me Dad always had a mean streak—she knew it before she married him—but she thought she could love it out of him." I closed my eyes, hating how hard life had been for her. "She was wrong, because he didn't want to change. And, for the record, I've never wanted to hit a woman in my life."

"I never thought you did."

My lips curled up. "Murphy's a different story. He likes to press my buttons."

She pressed her cheek against my chest. "Maybe not having a sibling was best."

I wrapped my arms around her. "Nah. Murph's an arse, but he's got my back, and I love him even when he is a shit. Just as I know he's always there for me. I'm right thrilled for Mil and him—he's going to be an awesome father because he cares so much about his family. He'll do right by them, raise strong, smart, good people."

"So will you, Jake. You're the best man I know."

"What I'm trying to tell you is my fears were just that: fears developed in a young kid's head." I pulled back and cupped Ryn's cheeks and stared into her eyes. "I want to have a baby with you, Lauryn. More than one. Heaps. A footy team at least."

"How many is that?" she asked, suspicion and joy building in her eyes.

"Fifteen."

"Jake!"

I chortled as I pulled her farther into the room. "So, it's all set. We'll have a baby or ten." I eased her back down onto the sumptuous silky coverlet. "Let's start now."

She wound her arms around my neck, snuggling her hips closer to mine. She reached up and bit my earlobe, just the way that made me crazy, before pressing her lips to my ear.

"I'm not getting pregnant today." Ryn smiled. "Or this week, month—probably not this year."

I stared down at her, mouth hanging open, looking like a lunatic. "Why in bloody hell not? From our first meeting, I knew how much kids meant to you."

She smiled as she brushed my hair off my forehead. "Two reasons. The first is I want to enjoy time with you—just us. Because, you, Jake, make me crave things. Like spontaneous sex in the kitchen and lots of snuggle time. I want to take trips with you—surf with you. All the things you've talked about. Because I realized what I *really* wanted was to be loved. And you love me."

"I do love you. Plan to prove it, but I'm a bit guffed at you going off my scripted plan." Still, what man doesn't like hearing his woman wants more sex?

"If we have a baby, I can't jump you in the living room when you wear those glasses." She shivered. "I can't wait to slide those off while I kiss my way from your jaw down your chest."

"I thought you didn't like me to wear my specs."

Ryn giggled. "I don't like *other* women to see you in your glasses. Kind of like you don't want men to see me in my fancy new string bikini you urged me to return." She raised her brows, and I dropped my head, thinking of my ballistic response to the tiny strips of fabric she'd planned to wear down to the beach when we'd arrived at our suite after a light lunch in the resort's café.

She sobered and cupped my cheeks in her hands. "I had to let Dez's family off because I didn't want them to come back later to haunt my relationship with you. I needed to move past them—past my past. Because what I feel for you, I've never felt before. And while it scares me, I know what we're building is right."

"I get it." And I did. Because I'd let go of Ryn's past with Dez. Sure, it might bother me from time to time, but Ryn was mine now—and forever.

"And, Jake, I'm not afraid to live your sexy rocker lifestyle. If you change your mind, and that's what you want. But I do plan to keep singing to my babies."

I leaned in and kissed her, loving the feel of her lips against mine, loving the feel of her ardent belief that she shared in the raising and loving of the children in her program. "We'll figure that part out as we go. Murphy, Hayden, and Flip are all on hiatus. If anything musical comes up, you and I will talk before the band does something new. Plus, I'm a grad student now—gotta make time for that."

She leaned her cheek against my chest, snuggling closer. "You're not mad at me anymore? I hated that you left like that after we talked to Detective Davenport. The whole flight here, I worried you'd break up with me."

"Blimey," I exclaimed, tugging her shoulders back to peruse her eyes. The truth and the fear lay bare there, easy to access.

"I was jealous. Heaps jealous, really. And I worried you didn't want me as I did you. So, in part, this trip is a bribe."

She frowned. "For?"

"To prove I'm good enough to be your bloke."

She laid her palm against my cheek, her thumb rubbing over

the days' old scruff there.

"Ah, Jake. I never once doubted you being good enough for me. I worried I wasn't enough for you."

She leaned up and kissed me, but I kept it short because I had more questions.

"Right-o. Much as I want to keep kissing you, you've a second reason for waiting on the nippers. Besides lots of shagging and holidays?"

She nodded, but this time her eyes looked a little more hesitant. She cleared her throat but met my gaze.

"I know it's old-fashioned and maybe even silly." She gathered up all her hair and pulled it into a knot, her way of keeping her hands busy when she was nervous. "I-I want to be married first."

I slid off the bed and stood. Ryn's eyes widened in panic when I took her hand and tugged her back toward the sliding door that led to our private beach. Likely, a journo would catch this, but no way I was letting Ryn hold on to any unnecessary worry or fear.

I opened the door and positioned her outside with a view of the soft, white sand and smooth, aquamarine water. "Stay right there."

I turned back into the room, grabbed one of the frangipani and the small black box from my luggage—just where I left it when I walked down to the beach earlier. I raced back to Ryn, whose face was caught between fear and desolation. Tears built in the corners of her eyes.

"Isaac told me you cursed."

She nodded, her face still etched with worry. "I was upset you left."

"That's when I knew," I said.

She raised her gaze to mine, asking me to elaborate without words.

"Knew you loved me as I love you. Whatever you were feeling was strong, see. And that my trip here needed to include one more important detail. Took me a while to find the right one." My cheeks heated. "That's why I wasn't at the police station like you asked."

I dropped to both my knees in front of her and handed her the delicate pink flower. She took it with trembling hands.

"Lauryn Jade Hudson, I love you, and I want to have babies with you—when you're ready. I love you because you sing lullabies like an angel and make sure those children will always love music, too. You work harder than anyone I know, and you draw me like no one else ever will."

I brought up my hand and opened the ring box. I'd never seen her engagement ring from Dez, and I knew Ryn would never compare the two. Still, I wanted this moment, our lifetime together, to be just that: *ours*. The ring I found for her was a square cut, three-carat diamond with half-carat sapphires on either side of the platinum setting. Fine smaller baguette diamonds slid down the sides of the delicate, rounded band.

"Malted Milk Duds," she whispered, her breath catching as she took in the ring. "It's…It's beautiful."

I smirked at the Laurynism. No matter what Murphy said, Lauryn would tame his foul mouth long before he was able to corrupt her. Because my woman's gentleness cloaked a will of steel tempered by past betrayals. She rose from the travesty of her childhood, from a messy first love, and came out both vulnerable and strong enough to love wholly—the way I loved her.

212

"I keep telling you you're beautiful to me, Lauryn. I love you. I can't imagine a day without speaking to you, hearing your voice raised in song. I want that for me and for our kids. Will you marry me? Here? On this island on Valentine's Day?"

"What?" Her eyes widened as she whispered the word.

My hands shook and the ring box grew slippery in my hand. "I-I w-want to m-m-marry you."

She dropped the flower I'd handed her, her eyes still wide, her mouth gaping slightly.

Not quite the reaction I expected. I took a deep breath and relaxed my throat, then my jaw. My heart rammed against my chest, but I managed to get the next words out with the clarity I usually took for granted. "You're my everything, Ryn. I don't want, will never want, anyone else to kiss, hold, laugh, and cry with. There's not another woman in the world I'd ever want to create a family with. Please. Marry me."

She sank to her knees in front of me and touched my cheek, her eyes skimming over my skin as lightly as her finger tips. "Oh, my…Jake." Her voice was a mere breath, not more than a whisper. "Yes. I'll marry you here. Now. Always."

I slid the ring on her finger and pressed a kiss there before I caught her by the back of the neck and brought her lips to mine.

First touch, I had the same thought as I did every time she kissed me: *heaven.*

EPILOGUE
Ryn

Cautious, plod-along Jake managed to surprise all of us. One of the calls he made after sending me to the beach was to the resort's concierge. Jake admitted, rubbing the back of his neck, that he asked the resort to provide an assortment of wedding gowns and flower options so I could pick out my favorite.

The simple spaghetti-strap sheath dress with a short train, all in a soft, ivory silk made me smile, as did the hair and makeup specialists who'd knocked on the door two days after he proposed.

He scrubbed his hands over his clean-shaven cheeks as he eyed the stylists parading into our room. "If you want a big wedding, we can wait."

I stepped into his arms and kissed him with the soft promise of more later. "I want this, here, between us. It's perfect."

He pulled me tighter to him, ignoring the women who were now blushing and smiling as they bustled around us. "I'll never, ever leave you."

Those words clinched my decision. Jake understood my need for certainty—not from the world but from him. And he offered it to me if I was brave enough to take it.

I was.

As twilight slid into moonrise, Jake led me down a tiki-torch lined path to the edge of the ocean. My bare feet sank into the soft, warm, white sand. A small arbor twined with native flowers and greenery stood at the end, two feet from the water. A smiling officiant stood there, along with two other hotel staff.

The moonlight on the water proved a magical backdrop to

the warm setting, softer, dreamier than I imagined. The perfect setting to marry the man who helped me find not just my way but my heart.

I turned to face him, my bouquet of frangipani fragrant, the lap of water a soft symphony, as the officiant began.

"Dearly beloved, we're gathered here to witness the joining of Jacob Etsam and Lauryn Hudson."

A thought, one I should have had sooner, burst from my lips: "Your mom! Is she going to be upset?"

Jake turned to grin at me. "Mum!"

One of the people I'd assumed was hotel staff stepped forward. She had tight gray curls and rosy cheeks. Her eyes twinkled with mischief and maybe—I hoped—pleasure as she hugged me tight. "Oh, my dear girl, I'm heaps thrilled to welcome you to the family. Murphy and Mila have told me so much about you—and how good you are for my Jakey."

I hugged her back tighter. "Thank you," I whispered. "Thank you for your son. I adore him."

She stepped back and wiped her eyes with an embroidered handkerchief. "I know. Just as he does you."

She turned to Jake. "You surprised us all with this, Jake, but I couldn't be prouder." She pulled him in for a hug and whispered something in his ear.

Jake grinned as he stepped back. He threaded his fingers through mine. During our exchange, a narrow slice of new moon rose from the ocean, the soft light draping us in its majesty.

We said our vows as a small group of singers sang an island song. I later learned it was a love song they sang at many local weddings. While I didn't understand the words, the emotions it

215

evoked settled around my shoulders, enveloping me further in this moment Jake created.

"I take thee, Jacob Milton Etsam, to be my husband."

Jake's smile turned lopsided and his eyes brightened as he replied, "I take thee, Lauryn Jade Hudson, to be my wife."

In that moment, I could see what my life would be like in five years, ten, even forty. Laughing, snuggling, singing—so much singing—art, poetry, shrieking kids, barking dogs, trips to beaches like this one.

And Jake. Always Jake. There for me, as he promised, standing at my side, holding me up, keeping me safe and filling me with love.

ACKNOWLEDGMENTS

As always, thank you, Chris. Your unwavering support and love shine through in all you do for the kids and me. I couldn't ask for a better man, and I'm thrilled to wake up with you each day.

To my family, thank you for your patience with my dream—and letting me hang out in my head *way* too often.

LERA ladies and gentlemen, thank you for being so supportive, for making me love writing again, and for sharing your knowledge so freely. You are the best.

To my AuthorLab writing pals: You keep me on task and keep me motivated. I love your commitment and passion. I love reading your posts and stories. And I love how diverse our group is.

To Deb, thank you for seeing the big picture—and making sure I see it, too.

To Nicole, thank you for the advice on Seattle, and for generally being awesome.

To my Divas, especially Jane—you kicked ass with the eARC's and I can never thank you enough.

To Clarissa, once again the cover is gorgeous. I love working with you.

And to my readers and reviewers. Thank you for your time. It's precious, and I'm so, so glad you spent some of it with me.

ABOUT THE AUTHOR

With a degree in international marketing and a varied career path that includes content management for a web firm, marketing direction for a high-profile sports agency, and a two-year stint with a renowned literary agency, Alexa Padgett has returned to her first love: writing fiction.

Alexa spent a good part of her youth traveling. From Budapest to Belize, Calgary to Coober Pedy, she soaked in the myriad smells, sounds, and feels of these gorgeous places, wishing she could live in them all—at least for a while. And she does in her books.

She lives in New Mexico with her husband, children, and Great Pyrenees pup, Ash. When not writing, schlepping, or volunteering, she can be found in her tiny kitchen, channeling her inner Barefoot Contessa.

Turn the page for a sneak peek at Chapter one of Deep in the Heart, the first book in a new contemporary romance series!

CHAPTER ONE
Jenna

The shop's outdated, brass doorbell tinkled, and I froze, my hands hovering over the small black keys of my laptop. Like most of the rest of the shop, the bell was a holdover from the mid-century remodeling that occurred back when Austin was a small town with country music roots—long before South by Southwest and even most of the hot live-music venues lined Sixth Street, located a mere block from my current seat.

I strained for another sound. My body tensed further, unwilling to move much like a rabbit who's scented a coyote.

That stupid little bell. Its sweet, tinkling chime remained an unusual occurrence, and one of the reasons I'd agreed to work with my Pop-pop. Interacting for hours on end with people exhausted me still. Even years after I'd been the unwitting—and unhappy—star witness in one of the largest trials in the country's history.

But that was years before. Bad people went to jail. I survived. Now, I flourished. I sighed, still slightly annoyed I'd run back to Austin, a town I'd run from, never planning to return.

Footsteps echoed through the front room, tapping a leisurely pace across the hardwood floors. Unfrozen muscles eased, and I swiped the fine layer of sawdust from my hands with one of Pop-pop's faded red flannel squares. A throwback to the Depression, he said, though why I wasn't quite sure. Pop-pop was born at the start of World War II, so it wasn't like the man lived through those days. Yet, even now, the man wouldn't toss anything—and I mean one little wrapper—if he thought he could reuse it someway.

My heart rate sped up as I rounded my work table, cursing

Pop-pop's doctor's appointment. I was even worse at customer service than I was at idle chitchat. But as the sole employee—correction, co-owner—in the building, my responsibility was to the customer. Didn't mean I had to like it.

I stumbled to a stop and I squeezed the cloth, trying hard not to hyperventilate. Of all the days…of all the people…dammit, *this* was why I'd attended college in Seattle. That and to prove to my family I was strong enough to be on my own.

"Ben," I said, my voice small. My shoulders folded in.

The look Ben gave me now caused shudders to roll up my spine. He swiveled around to face me, his whiskey-brown eyes widening then narrowing as a smirk drifted over those perfect, sculpted lips.

"Hey, there, little girl," he drawled. I hated his drawl near as much as the fact he'd called me "little girl" since high school. "Heard tell you were in some music magazine."

"Not the first time," I shot back. The thing about Ben was to never show fear. Never back down. He craved the rush of overpowering me emotionally, physically.

He leaned in, a small smirk gracing those lips. "So I was told. But, see, none of the old crowd knew you were back."

My heart thumped in a painful, erratic rhythm against my ribs. That was intentional. I didn't want to hang around Ben or Robbie or any of the other shallow people I'd surrounded myself with all those years before.

I gripped the piece of flannel even tighter in my fist as I threw my shoulders back, giving him my haughtiest stare down. Not that easy to do when he was a good six inches taller than me.

"You saw me. Now, will you please leave?" I asked.

His eyes darkened and his lips collapsed into an angry sneer. Much more the Ben I remembered.

"Don't think I will just yet, Princess. I want to see more, and I'm the customer, so you need to help me find what I'm looking for." He missed my glare because he glanced around, his lip curling as he eyed the small shop. Of course, Ben, being the preppy baseball player he was—wanted to believe he still was—wouldn't recognize the quality or value of the instruments surrounding him…either in monetary value or in prestige. Just walking into this shop was a privilege many musicians longed for—but couldn't afford.

Ben, like Robbie and the rest of the people I used to hang out with—used to consider important—knew nothing of this world. He lived baseball. Had all through high school and college, too. Both boys' dedication to the sport meant I spent little time with my boyfriend during our senior year.

Robbie's work earned him the starting position at second base at the University of Texas while Ben typically rode the bench. I'd heard through a convoluted grapevine that Ben was cut from his minor league team this year, which explained his sudden interest in me.

He'd always needed someone else to beat up on to feel good.

Why had I ever hung out with this guy?

Because he was best friends with my boyfriend—the only boy I could see, would ever love…all that lame shit so common in sixteen-year-old girls who hadn't lived enough to know better. Know anything, really.

The years I'd put into this shop, my reputation, mattered. I was proud to work here, proud that people wanted one of my guitars. Proud to be written up in some of the top industry magazines and the shelf of awards I accrued.

"I can't believe I once screwed someone who works in a guitar shop. I thought, with your parents and your looks, you'd actually accomplish something with your life, Jenna. These are nice," Ben said, pulling me out of my daydream where I kicked him in the crotch. "For instruments. I should get one."

I swallowed back the snort. No way Ben could afford one of these instruments. More importantly, my grandfather would never sell one to Ben.

"Why isn't there a price tag?" Ben asked.

"Because it's a custom-made guitar that took six months to build."

Ben raised his eyebrows and gestured at it. "Are you saying I can't afford it?"

"Most of these are spoken for," I said, refusing to be drawn into a verbal sparring match. Those exhausted me almost as much as being nice to Ben.

The bell tinkled again.

Really?

Twice in less than ten minutes. This barrage of people was *not* okay.

I needed to hire someone to handle all this.

I blinked away the dizziness. I needed to eat. I needed my pills. I needed to get into my workshop and away from Ben, and the ugly memories he evoked.

"Look, we really don't have anything in common anymore," I said. "As you just pointed out. I make guitars, and you want to play pro ball." Best to pretend I didn't know he'd been cut. That would just make him meaner. And harder to get rid of.

"We're like…corn and toads," I finished. That didn't make much sense. Half of what I said didn't make sense, especially when I was stressed.

I finally caught a glimpse of the new customer. Tall. Taller than Ben and broader, too. His dark hair was short on the sides but tousled on top. His slightly ratty T-shirt hugged him tighter than a jealous lover. Most of the time, tight tees meant men with big egos. Not my thing.

He turned toward me, and I sucked in a breath, squeezing that piece of flannel as if it alone would keep me upright. Holy shit on sugar toast, this man was *pretty*.

No. That was the wrong word. His eyes, a much warmer though lighter brown than Ben's, caught mine and held. I'd already cataloged the rest of his face: couple days of scruff shadowed his firm chin and square jaw, full lips—not as full as Ben's bee-stung ones—slashing dark brows and warm tanned skin tone. The bridge of his nose thickened in the same way my older brother Jude's had after he'd broken it in a football accident ten years ago.

"Hey. I'm talking to you." Ben grabbed my wrist, yanking me forward.

"I'm done listening." I twisted my arm, trying to wriggle from his hold. Ben's fingers tightened to the point of numbing my fingers. He leaned forward into my personal space and used my captured hand to pull me forward until my chest was practically laying on the wood counter. Nope, nope, nope.

I gripped the bat I'd leaned against the counter, hefting it as I brought it forward, the end shoving hard against Ben's chest.

"I said I'm done."

He squeezed my wrist tighter and leaned into the bat. "We're finished when *I* say—"

Sweet baby Jesus in a peach tree. I heft the bat better, planning to take a swing.

"What's going on here?" The man asked. His voice, all gravelly and rich, washed over me. "You all right there, miss?"

I yanked my arm, twisting, as I shoved the bat harder into Ben's chest. Ben let go of me, and I stumbled back. My piece of flannel dropped to the counter.

"You need to go," I said.

Ben scowled at my look, so I turned my attention to the second man. My gaze locked on my new customer, trying to place him. He was older than me by a few years—in his late twenties, early thirties, I'd bet—and his jeans were worn in that sexy, I-work-hard way no type of washing could replicate. Now that he faced me, I saw his T-shirt said ARMY. An *excellent* look for him, especially when paired with—swoon!—scuffed motorcycle boots.

Who was he? I should know him; I knew I should.

His gaze never wavered from mine but, somehow, I experienced his awareness to the rest of the store. He stepped forward again, getting between Ben and me.

His gait hitched. As if he had a stiff leg. While uneven, he had the tread of a predator. Too young for the arthritis Pop-pop fought off each morning. I shivered with delicious anticipation for his voice.

"Y'all good here?" the dark-eyed man said.

I flinched at the bite in his tone. I hadn't done anything wrong. Wait, now the stranger glared at Ben.

"Hey, there. What can I help you with?"

"You being harassed?"

I plastered on a smile, deciding to stick to honey instead of the vinegar I wanted to spew all over Ben. "I was, but I sorted it all out. Everything's fine. Do you have an appointment?"

"Yep. I'm here to meet with the younger Olsen 'bout a new guitar."

"Looking at her," I said, shooting for the upbeat personality most people expected me to wear.

The guy's brows drew together tight, and he shook his head. "Huh. Didn't expect a woman. Got the sense from your…grandfather?" At my nod, he continued, "Got the sense I would be meeting someone older. And nowhere near as pretty." This was said with a smile.

"I'm Jenna." I stuck out my hand, and the man clasped it in his larger hand. His palm was rough, almost abrasive. Not that mine were the soft white wonders they'd been while I was at Northern University. No, my hands now were used to cut, shape and smooth wood, work I found soothing.

He turned my hand and studied the redness from Ben's harsh treatment of my wrist.

"You do this to the gal here?" he asked in a low rumble that sounded like trouble.

Shocker of shocks, I *liked* this man's hand touching mine. Like, a lot. Strange, especially after my rejection of Ben. Ben's gaze bored into the side of my head, and my cheeks flushed at both men's continued scrutiny.

"I asked you a question," he said to Ben. His voice was deep, near as rough as his palm. I liked that, too. Mainly because he sounded nothing like Ben.

"I don't owe you nothing," Ben said, sullen but also wary like he, too, was trying to place this man.

"My body guard's outside," he said, tilting his head back a little. "Should I get him?"

"You are the country music star, Camden Grace." Ben smiled like a bright penny. "What are you doing here?"

That's where I'd seen him—practically everywhere since I'd returned to the city. Camden Grace was Austin's hometown darling. Born on a ranch just west of Lake Travis, Camden Grace had crooned his way to the top of the country charts by his mid-twenties. His first album had to be…oh…five years ago. Since then, he'd strummed out a dozen multi-platinum singles and two more full-length albums, and, in the last couple of weeks, some bad press.

"Need a new guitar," Camden rumbled. "J. Olsen's are the best."

My fingers tingled as my hand slipped from Camden's. I clenched my fist, trying to ignore my attraction. To Camden Grace. Pile up the pepperoni and dive right in; I was always attracted to the *worst* of the male species.

"I love your music, sir." Ben's voice took on the excitement of a small, yappy puppy.

"Can't say I like your treatment of Miss Olsen here much," Cam grunted. "Why don't you skedaddle before you get yourself in a heap of trouble?"

Ben's scowl returned. Uh oh. I knew that look. Ben didn't take well to being ordered around. He'd always been the Bantam rooster in our circle, needing to preen and peck away at others to keep himself at the top of the hen house. I'd have to watch out for Ben's retaliation, which would be swift…and cause me more emotional distress. My hand gripped my bat tighter.

"I didn't see you on the schedule," I said in a rush, trying to diffuse the situation before Ben could escalate it and cost us business. "But I'm glad to walk you through your options, Mr. Grace."

He leaned his hip against the counter and crossed his arms over his broad chest. Standing there, he dwarfed Ben. But it wasn't just the size difference. There was a watchfulness in Camden's eyes, an awareness of danger that Ben, with his soft, privileged life, would never have.

"Cam's fine."

"Right." I turned back to Ben. "I'll need to ask you to leave so I can work with my client."

Ben scowled deeper, his hands clenching into fists.

Cam dipped his head to acknowledge a large man now peering through the glass. Sunglasses covered his eyes but his scowl meant no-nonsense. His brown hair was buzzed short, and his arms showed off well-defined biceps.

The man opened the door and strode in like he owned the place. "You all right?" he asked Cam. He sounded like a bear—even deeper and growlier than Cam and without that melodic quality.

"This man doesn't want to leave the premises even though the lady's asked so nicely."

I dropped my gaze and bit the inside of my lip to keep from smiling. Polite might be as far as I'd take my request. Nice shouldn't signify—in part because Ben never deserved kindness. Not from me, anyway.

Ben's scowl grew as he looked between us. "I'm going. I'll be back."

"I hope not," I said. "In fact, I'd prefer not to see you again."

Ben scowled. "We have unfinished business."

I turned back to Cam, ignoring Ben. "So, what are you looking for, Mr...um, Cam?"

My shoulders unbunched when Ben strode from the shop, the door slamming loud enough to make me jump. Cam's bodyguard wandered forward, placing himself near the glass door, I was sure so that Ben knew he was being watched.

"Not your favorite person?" he asked.

Man, that rough voice sent shivers up and down my spine. Tingles upon tingles that danced just right across my skin. I scowled to cover my reaction.

"Let's focus on your guitar."

"It's not my business," Cam said. He ran his index finger over the redness around my wrist. "And I get you don't want me to pursue him being here further, but he hurt you."

My gaze slammed back to his, eyebrows arched in shock.

"Fear rolled off you when I stepped in here. You don't like him."

I shrugged, unwilling to comment on my nonexistent relationship to a stranger—more, a rich and famous customer. "I don't."

"You need anything else, Cam?" the bodyguard asked.

Cam raised his eyebrows at me. When I didn't answer, he said, "I think we're okay now, Chuck. Just...keep an eye out, will ya?"

"I'll hang out here."

"I'll get you a chair," I said as I turned toward the back. I still gripped my bat. I set it down in the corner, trying to be unobtrusive.

"No need, ma'am."

My steps stuttered at the address—I was twenty-four! I couldn't be a ma'am yet. Whatever. More significant issues to focus on, Jenna. Like staying calm. Icing my throbbing wrist.

"You sure?" I asked.

Chuck nodded. He turned toward the door and crossed his arms. While he looked relaxed, his eyes continued to rove across the parking lot. With his big body, short hair and all-seeing eyes, I'd bet he was former military.

I ran my hands down my thighs and closed my eyes, taking a moment to realign my world—and my place in it.

"Want to come on back, Mr. Grace?"

"Told you, it's Cam. And sure. My leg's not interested in standing today."

"Oh! I'm so sorry! I saw you limping…"

"Shrapnel. From a bomb in the sandlot." At my look of askance, he said, "Iraq."

Golly gee green jelly beans. He played guitar and he was a wounded war vet? I'd missed plenty of details about Camden Grace—probably because I'd never been that into country music even when I lived here during high school.

"You were in the army?"

He raised a brow. "Army Ranger at your service, ma'am." His scowl darkened. "Honorably discharged, though, thanks to my bum leg." For the first time, he appeared uncertain, lost even. "Been a long time now."

I motioned him to the back and he moved slower this time, concentrating on each step from his right leg.

"Bad, then? The shrapnel?" I said, gesturing to his leg.

"Took out a chunk of muscle. Never going to win any beauty contests."

I held out a chair and he settled in, wincing. I wasn't so sure—he was beautiful. But he was also a customer, and Ben's physical attacked created a severe case of freaking out…which, come to think of it, I hadn't done any of since we started talking. Huh.

I pulled another piece of flannel from my back pocket and twisted it. I needed to take my pills.

I blinked, then flushed. "I'm sorry. I didn't hear you."

"That's the second time you've gotten that look in your eye. What did that flannel ever do to you?"

I laughed, but it was a flat, hollow sound.

"You going to tell me if I need to beat up that kid who was in here before? What I saw—he harassed you."

This time, I smiled with actual warmth. "No, but thank you. Ben and I have a history."

"Got that. What I don't get is why you didn't kick him in the balls like you wanted to."

"It's not his balls I want to drop kick to Saturn," I said, mostly to myself. "That leaves too much of him here."

"Ah. There's a bit of humor. Sass suits you."

"Right." I cleared my throat and settled into my desk, pulling out a paper and pad. "So. A new guitar?"

Cam scratched his cheek, the whiskers on his cheek making a raspy sound. "Yeah. I busted the last one."

"Well, if you bring it in, we can repair it."

The ruddy stain or embarrassment crept up his neck and crested his cheeks. "Not this one. I-ah-smashed it."

I jerked back, my mouth falling slack. Pop-pop's guitars

were expensive, even for a wealthy country singer. Dropping ten grand—or more—to bust a guitar, especially one as beautiful as my grandfather's, was a shame.

"On purpose?"

"Things got a little carried away on the bus, and I took out my temper on the guitar."

He pronounced it the Texan way: gi-tar. I liked that, too. Oddly. I wasn't much for an accent of any kind, preferring the men I dated to be as vanilla as possible. Not that I'd dated much—at all—since I'd lived in Seattle. Being a star witness in a trial is hard on anonymity. Being the woman who slept with the drug dealer....I hadn't known Charles dealt drugs at the time, but that really didn't make me look any better in the media.

My hand shook, and I blinked multiple times, trying to keep my mind here, in the present.

No good.

Pre-pills was not the time to think about love, romance, and the lack of sex in my life.

I dug around in my purse and pulled out my pill case. I dumped the two capsules in my hand before dropping them onto my tongue. I opened my yogurt smoothie and drank most of it down along with the pills.

Cam watched me, questions building in his eyes. I ignored them as I placed my pill box back in my purse and then shut my purse into my desk drawer.

"That bothers you. Me busting the instrument."

"Yes," I said.

He rubbed his hand over his lip and swung his left leg forward and back, like a pendulum. I kept my gaze fixed there, unable to meet his eyes.

"I'm not violent. Usually."

I picked up my pencil and tapped it on my pad in front of me. "This new instrument. Got any idea what you're interested in?"

"First I need to address your concerns." He waited until I looked him in the eye. "I found out my father died."

"I'm sorry," I whispered.

"I handled the news poorly. He and I…" Cam sighed, dropped his gaze and rubbed the back of his neck. "As you said, my father and I had a history. Not all good. If it makes you feel any better, I regret my reaction. I regret busting my guitar, and I regret having to call your grandfather to tell him what I did."

"Okay."

"Buried my father two weeks ago. Held my mother through the funeral."

What to say? No words came.

Cam sighed. "All right. Down to business. Something flashy. It's going to be my new stage guitar." A smile tugged at the corner of his lips. "I've been asked to perform at Fort Bliss. For the Fourth of July concert they're putting together."

I'd read an article about Camden Grace headlining the Soldier Celebration tour. All the proceeds from the event went to war veterans and their families. I approved of that cause. But one of the reporters sniped earlier this week that the performance was supposed to help rebuild Cam's deteriorating reputation. "That's in just a few weeks."

His eyebrow shot up and there was the entitled jerk the world loved to hate. "That a problem?"

I sat up straighter, met his eye. "Yes," I said. "I'm booked."

He leaned in a little closer as he smiled, flashing those damn adorable dimples as his eyes lit up. Confidence. Best aphrodisiac ever.

Of course, he knew he was hella sexy. The man graced magazine covers, billboards.

"Your grandfather spoke highly of your skill, your work ethic. Said if anyone could make me a guitar that sings sweeter than Faith Hill, it was you."

"It's not a question of if I can make you a custom guitar," I began.

"Actually, it is."

He leaned in a little closer. I smelled caramel as his warm breath slid over my skin.

"Unfortunately, creating a quality instrument is a process," I managed to say without growling. I'd just dealt with Ben. No way I was letting another man push me around. "My *name* is attached to your instrument. I only allow the highest quality to leave this building."

Cam settled back on his stool and eyed my hands. "I understand a need for perfection." His gaze rose to mine and the heat in his eyes slammed back through me. "Me, I'm all about it. In fact, that drives my team crazy." He settled his elbows on his thighs and leaned forward again, using that sexy-as-sin face to his advantage. "This is about what your pop-pop said you could do for me. And the fact I'm looking for a perfect-for-me instrument that I plan to boast about at my concert and for the rest of my career. So, question is, can you help me out so I can help you out?"